MAKING SEAKER
KAREN AUTIO

GP | CRWTH PRESS

Library and Archives Canada Cataloguing in Publication

Title: Making Seaker / Karen Autio.
Names: Autio, Karen, author.
Identifiers: Canadiana (print) 20210200065 | Canadiana
(ebook) 20210200073 | ISBN 9781989724095
(softcover) | ISBN 9781989724125 (EPUB)
Classification: LCC PS8601.U85 M35 2021 | DDC jC813/.6—dc23

Copy edited by Dawn Loewen
Proofread by Audrey McClellan
Cover and interior design by Julia Breese

Published by

Crwth Press
#204 – 2320 Woodland Drive
Vancouver, BC V5N 3P2
www.crwth.ca

Printed and bound in Canada

*All stories are connected, new ones
woven from the threads of the old.*
—ROBIN WALL KIMMERER, *Braiding Sweetgrass*

CHAPTER ONE

"Can I wait until fall to start school, Mom? I won't learn anything now." It's the first Friday of June and Jamie Sola's heart is thumping at lightspeed.

"You'll be fine," says Mom, arranging bread for a sandwich on the counter. "With three weeks left of the school year, you might make a friend before summer."

Jamie rolls her eyes. *Mom doesn't get it. I probably won't even make a friend before winter.* Jamie shoves a spoonful of cereal into her mouth and grinds it to mush.

"Turkey or salami?" Mom asks. Her messy bun has so many light brown hairs sticking out, it looks like the Sputnik satellite.

"Salami."

Mom adds the meat to the sandwich.

1

Jamie asks, "How many people live here?"

"Around seventeen hundred." Mom tucks the sandwich into a reusable container. "Your school has about one hundred fifty students."

Jamie slumps. *With those numbers, I won't make a friend before high school.* The cereal feels as heavy as cement in her stomach. She plunks her bowl in the sink. "If I stay home I can help you finish unpacking."

Mom's glare is clear—Jamie has to go.

She dawdles brushing her teeth. In her bedroom, Jamie opens her box of models. She carefully pulls out the lunar lander she built. At her old school in Sault Ste. Marie, the grade 4 boys were okay with her as a quiet science nerd. But no girl invited her over until halfway through the year. And that was only because Liisa Halonen was new and shyer than Jamie. *If only my lunar lander could blast off and take me back to Sault Ste. Marie.*

"Jamie," Mom calls, "your lunch is ready. Off you go."

Jamie sets the model on her dresser, then returns to the kitchen to get her lunch bag. Her little brother, Brock, jumps up from his Lego construction site to give her a tight hug. *It's so weird how he*

2

got Dad's dark brown hair and Mom's blue eyes, and I got her light brown hair and Dad's hazel eyes. I gotta look up how genes work later.

The walk to school is less than four blocks. Jamie heads off fifteen minutes before the bell.

A chipmunk darts across the driveway, tail straight up like an antenna. It vanishes into a crack in the stone wall. Maybe she could train this chipmunk like the one at Liisa's. It would snatch peanuts-in-the-shell right out of their hands. One time it stuffed three in its cheeks.

School crashes back into Jamie's thoughts. Her tummy churns as she strolls along the side of the road.

The bell rings as Jamie reaches the school. She finds the grade 4/5 classroom upstairs, and there are only twenty desks. She looks around wondering where to sit. The fiftieth-anniversary moon landing poster on the far wall prompts a tiny smile.

A desk near the poster has a big hand-drawn card on it that says, "Welcome, Jamie Sola." Jamie sits and opens the card. It's been signed by lots of kids. Jamie guesses these are her new classmates.

A couple of girls arrive, chatting away. *I should say hi.*

3

The blonde one sits to Jamie's right and pulls a notebook out of the desk. It has the name Beth Anderson in green marker on the cover, surrounded by blue-and-green doodles.

I really should say hi.

Beth's ponytail flicks around as she talks nonstop to the girl with darker skin and high cheekbones she calls Raina. Her glossy black hair is in a ponytail too, and she has a loud laugh. Down the spine of the binder on her desk are neatly printed red block letters that spell RAINA LAROUCHE.

Jamie's legs vibrate. When the desks are filled, there are seven girls, including Jamie, and thirteen boys.

Mr. Pratter is tall with ginger hair, and his voice sounds kind. He introduces Jamie but doesn't make her stand or say anything. *My favourite teacher ever.*

"Beth, you're Jamie's first-day buddy."

Jamie catches Beth's eye and smiles. Beth pushes her glasses higher on her nose and doesn't smile back.

When announcements are done, Mr. Pratter says, "Beth, now's a good time to take Jamie on a tour."

Beth bolts from the room and Jamie has to run to catch up. As they race past each class, Beth rattles off the grade and teacher's name. She speaks so quietly, Jamie can barely hear her.

Mom always says be friendly to make friends. Ask questions. Jamie asks, "What's your favourite subject?"

"Writing."

"What do you like to write?"

"Stories."

"What about?"

"Animals."

Being friendly is SO hard.

Following Beth, Jamie gets a peek at the gym with its bright blue floor. Then Beth darts out the door, saying something about the Ojibwe language room and the big open area with tables and benches.

Did she say that's where everyone eats or meets? "What did—?"

"Presumably you've seen the office already," Beth says, "so we'll go downstairs."

After a flying tour of the basement, they're back upstairs and at their desks. Math is in progress. Beth groans and pulls out her textbook. Jamie's stomach finally relaxes as she dives into math problems. Numbers are predictable and understandable. No emotions. Answers are right or wrong. *Ahh.*

Jamie is ravenous by nutrition break and inhales her granola bar. Beth talks with Raina, the girl with the dark ponytail—something about pancakes also being called hotcakes and crepes. Jamie wouldn't be able to get a word in even if she were the kind of kid who'd try. The pair of grade 5 girls sits at the front of the classroom, and the other girls in grade 4 huddle at the back.

To Jamie, the fifteen minutes feel like an hour. But the activity break outside feels even longer. Jamie wanders around the playground, then up the hill to the trees. She leans against a rough, warm trunk until the bell rings.

One hundred more minutes of Jamie saying nothing.

At lunch break, she sets her containers of food out on her desk. Solo meal ahead for Jamie Sola— no huddling with a friend for her.

Mr. Pratter glances at Jamie, then says to Beth, "Miss Anderson, did you forget to show Jamie the lunchroom?"

Beth flicks her blue eyes toward Jamie. She mumbles, "No, I showed her." Beth grabs her lunch bag and whispers, "Coming?"

Jamie feels her cheeks flush. That's what she'd missed hearing. She gathers her meal and rushes after Beth and Raina.

Will Beth invite me to sit with them?

She doesn't, so Jamie takes a spot at the empty table next to theirs. She busies herself with eating and trying not to stare at anyone.

Three boys from their class saunter toward Beth. The one with short blond hair and wide shoulders tugs her ponytail. "How's it going, *Buddy Beth*?" The boys laugh.

"It was *awesome*, before *you* got here," Raina snaps, and the guys head to a far table.

Wow—she definitely isn't shy around boys.

"Jeremy *thinks* he's so hilarious," Beth mutters to Raina. "But mostly he's mean and obnoxious. I'm glad you got rid of him."

Note: Stay out of Jeremy's orbit.

A rascal of younger boys fills up Jamie's table. Rascal—a perfect word she learned from Dad. He's a fan of uncommon collective nouns—swell of surfers, worship of writers, scurry of squirrels.

Jamie eats quickly, packs her lunch bag and returns to her desk, even though everyone's supposed to go outside. She pulls out her cell phone and texts Liisa about her awful first day. Then Jamie uses the school Wi-Fi to check what the Perseverance rover has been up to on Mars.

All afternoon, Jamie never says a word or raises her hand. She only nods when Mr. Pratter checks if she understands what to do. Loading her backpack at dismissal, she's slower than an elderly sloth. She waits for the class to leave so she won't have to talk to anyone. No one waves to her except her teacher. All Liisa texts back is: **Horrible.** 😟

Jamie trudges home.

CHAPTER TWO

On Saturday morning, Jamie drags the box of models over beside her dresser. She stands her castle next to her lunar lander. Running her fingers along the "stone" wall, she remembers the thrill of gluing the pieces together as the medieval structure took shape.

Jamie picks up the boat, her first project. It's a model of a famous Viking ship. Grandma and Grandpa gave it to her for Christmas in grade 3. Jamie can spot all the flaws. She's better at building now.

"Jamie, let's go," calls Dad.

She and her family climb in their truck, and they drive downtown.

"Wow!" Jamie gapes at the larger-than-life statue of an Indigenous man in a birchbark canoe.

It's perched on a hill in Paddle-to-the-Sea Park behind the Nipigon Public Library. "It's bigger than I expected."

"And there are two more playgrounds at the marina," Dad boasts.

Jamie grins at her father. He sounds so proud talking about his hometown. When Dad got the job in Nipigon, he told the family about this park that's based on the classic book *Paddle-to-the-Sea* by Holling Clancy Holling. Dad brought home a copy of the book, and he and Jamie took turns reading it to Brock. In the story, a boy carves a small wooden man in a canoe and names the carving Paddle-to-the-Sea (which the author shortens to Paddle). Jamie loved reading about Paddle's journey floating all the way to the sea from near this town.

Dad parks their truck.

"I'm going up there first." Brock points to the canoe. He jumps out, leaving his door wide open. Dashing over to the hill, he climbs the steps leading to the seated paddler.

By the time Jamie reaches the sidewalk, Brock's swaying inside the boat. He clutches the sides. "Me and Paddle are swooshing down the creek."

"Hang on tight," Jamie calls.

But her brother's already climbing out. He runs down the stairs and stumbles on the bottom one yet manages not to fall. Soon he's squealing as Mom chases him around the two small lighthouses in the nearby play area. Jamie feels a wave of relief that her family has the park to themselves.

The shallow water in the "creek" cascades down the hill and empties into a pond shaped like Lake Superior, the largest Great Lake. Jamie swishes her hand around in the water, creating an eddy. *How many whirlpools did Paddle meet on his route?*

"Dad, is *Paddle-to-the-Sea* true?"

"No, it's fiction," says Dad, "but come look at this map."

She stands next to Dad at the huge sign. The map shows the five Great Lakes with Canada in the north and the United States in the south.

"The places in the story exist, though. Paddle started here, above Nipigon." Dad traces the route on the map. "Then the currents carried him southwest to Duluth, Minnesota, and through the Great Lakes to the Atlantic Ocean."

Jamie wishes the story were true.

She and Dad join Mom, who's watching Brock try out the metal slide.

Two girls arrive and scramble up the climbing dome.

"Those girls look about your age," Mom says.

"Yeah." Jamie's hands grow clammy as she recognizes Beth and Raina. "They're in my class."

"Go say hi."

Jamie takes three steps toward the girls.

Then she freezes. *They don't want to talk to me.* Her heart jackhammers as she turns and ducks into the play area that looks like a marsh. She weaves between tall metal bulrushes. Finding a life-sized heron, she strokes its neck.

Jamie peeks at the girls. They're laughing. *Did they see me?* She dips her head so her long hair falls forward to hide her burning cheeks. Jamie walks over to her family at the big grey-and-red grain ship.

Brock is *arrrr*ing like a pirate. Then he says, "Can we go see the playgrounds at the marmina?"

"I think you mean 'marina,'" Dad says. "Don't you want to play longer here?"

"Nope."

Jamie glances at the girls. "I want to go too."

Dad shrugs. "All right."

Jamie scurries behind the lighthouses to avoid

12

Beth and Raina on her way to the truck.

It takes only a few minutes to drive to the marina. As soon as the truck stops, Brock bolts to the playground zip line. The bar to grab is stuck halfway along the track. He jumps but he's nowhere near touching it. Jamie's tall enough to hop up so her fingertips can slide the bar to the platform for him.

Brock darts up the stairs. He grips the handles and pushes off, then stalls in the middle. Brock swings his legs but hardly budges.

Dad asks, "Want me to zip you across?"

"Yeah!" He shrieks as Dad rockets him along the track.

Jamie turns toward the highway bridge in the distance. Its three towers soar above the trees. They support the cables that hold up the bridge across the Nipigon River, like a giant triangular spiderweb. She pictures the map of the Great Lakes and twists her mouth to one side. *It's a long, long way to the ocean.*

"Mom, could a model boat travel all the way to the ocean from here, like in the story?"

"Yes, the water system is all connected," Mom says, "but it would be two thousand kilometres—maybe double that with currents and waves."

Jamie points south toward Lake Superior. "Could it get through the ship locks at Sault Ste. Marie?"

"I don't see why not."

Jamie swoops her arms. "What if a mega-storm washed it ashore where nobody lives?"

"That would be a problem."

"Would a model boat get smashed in Niagara Falls?" Her fragile Viking ship wouldn't survive a drop of even a metre.

"It would have to be tough to make it through the falls."

Dad calls, "I'm starving. Let's eat." He sets their cooler on a picnic table near the river.

Jamie shares a bench with Dad. He pulls left-over pepperoni pizza and cans of root beer out of the cooler. Everyone grabs a wedge of pizza.

The warm breeze rustles the poplar leaves and tickles Jamie's scalp. At the dock, a large blue-and-white boat is being tied up. Men clamber off hauling duffel bags, fishing rods and big coolers.

After the family's done eating and Brock has tossed a hundred pebbles into the river, they return to the truck and head home. As they drive past lawns exploding with clover and wild daisies, Jamie can't stop thinking about Paddle and his journey.

CHAPTER THREE

As soon as Jamie gets home, she grabs a pencil and pad of paper from her desk. What shape would work best? She sits cross-legged on the floor, sketching.

Humph. She wads the paper and throws it at her recycling bin. Misses.

Draws again.

Crumples, tosses, gets it in.

Jamie opens her model-building book. She hunts for boat designs and finds two. One is too basic. Design two is an ultra-fancy display-only ship. Even if it could float, it would sink in rough water in less than five minutes.

She tries a new angle. No good.

More attempts. Her recycling bin overflows and the floor is littered with ruined sketches.

Maybe a model boat is a bad idea. Last fall, she brought her lunar lander to show her class. Girls made fun of her and called her Looney Lander. None of them wanted to hang out with a model builder like Jamie.

By the time Liisa arrived, Jamie was ready to do anything to have a friend, so she acted exactly like Liisa. She pretended to hate science and math and to love shopping for clothes. Maybe that would work here. She could pretend she's Beth's twin.

It would be my Make-a-Friend project.

What do I know about Beth so far? Jamie writes down her observations.

1. ponytail
2. no nail polish (glad I don't have to wear it either)
3. blue eyes + wears glasses
4. loves writing, esp. animal stories (tough, but I can fake this)
5. blue and green fave colours
6. hates being first-day buddy (or being mine)
7. loves big words
8. doesn't like math (ugh, this one's hard)

9. likes pancakes
10. climbs to the top of the climbing dome at the park
11. quiet voice and laugh

*
**

On Monday morning, Jamie fastens her hair in a ponytail and chooses a blue T-shirt. Brock is starting junior kindergarten—JK—today. She could walk to school with him and Mom, but what if that backfires on her Make-a-Friend project? Jamie heads off early.

School begins with social studies. Mr. Pratter instructs the grade 5s, then grade 4s. On the Smart Board he shows a list of societies, like ancient Greece, medieval China and matriarchal First Nations. The project, due Monday, is to pick one, research daily life and social organization and compare with how we live. "Work in groups of two or three. Jamie, you can join Beth and Raina."

Here goes.

Beth sits up straight and tightens her ponytail. "I want to write about a First Nation."

"Me too," says Jamie, speaking softly. "I'm excited

17

to write about how people live." Beth smiles and hope flutters in Jamie's heart.

"Yes to that. Ojibwe, of course," Raina says, pointing to herself, "but it would be way more fun to draw maps. Around the edges we can show how my people used to live, with pictures of our homes and how we dressed."

Uh-oh. Jamie prefers Raina's idea. But if she says so, Beth won't want to be her friend.

Jamie pulls in a huge breath. "Could we do both?"

"Fine with me," Raina says, "as long as I don't have to do the writing."

"Jamie, do you like writing?" asks Beth.

"Yeah," Jamie lies, swallowing hard.

"Then you do all the writing," Beth says. "And Raina can do the drawing. I'll do more of the research."

Jamie says, "Okay," but her insides squirm. *I'm doomed.*

"I'll edit your work, Jamie," Beth adds. "Even the best writers need editing."

They settle down with their assigned laptops, each with different research topics to tackle. Research is the easy part.

They've already made great progress when Mr. Pratter tells them to return the laptops to the cart and take out their math textbooks.

Beth whispers, "Ugh. Math is abominable."

"I know," Jamie agrees. She forces herself to work slowly, as if she's struggling.

At lunch, Raina warmly says, "Come sit with us, Jamie." Her eyes are so dark, it's hard to see where the pupil ends and the iris begins.

This is the offer Jamie's been waiting for, but she can't keep herself from asking, "Are you sure?"

"Of course. Right, Beth?"

Beth shrugs.

Jamie grabs her lunch and follows them. The two friends sit across from each other at one end of a table. Jamie climbs over the bench and parks herself beside Beth.

Raina groans. "Mom made egg salad *again*. Soggy bread is so disgusting."

"I love egg salad," Jamie fibs. "Wanna trade?"

"Any day." Raina swaps sandwiches. "Thanks."

Jamie tries to swallow the egg-mayo mush and gags. She coughs to cover it up.

"You all right?" Beth asks.

"Went down the wrong way." *Any way is the*

wrong way. Jamie eats the rest as fast as she can and guzzles her juice box.

Beth says to Raina, "Too bad you couldn't come rescue us yesterday. You could've shooed that creepy bat out of our house in no time." She shudders. "Like that spooky bird you helped us with. It took us forever to get rid of the bat."

"Aww," says Raina. "I hope you didn't hurt it."

"Not until my mom accidentally knocked it onto the counter with the broom—"

"No!" Raina covers her mouth with both hands. "Was the bat okay?"

"I think it was only stunned," says Beth, wincing. "Mom trapped it in a shoebox and released it outside."

"I wish I could've been there to keep the bat safe." Raina munches Jamie's yummy ham and cheese sandwich.

In that nanosecond of silence, Jamie blurts, "So that was a shoooobox?" She giggles. "Get it? S-h-o-o…"

Beth gives her a slow blink.

Jamie's grin evaporates.

CHAPTER FOUR

On Tuesday morning, Mr. Pratter announces, "All students going to the district track and field meet next Wednesday have practice today during block 2. That's everyone who placed first or second last week."

Raina fist-bumps Beth.

The teacher continues, "The rest of you will join the grade sixes for a softball game."

Cheers outnumber the few boos.

On their way to collect their laptops from the cart, Jamie asks Beth, "Did you win an event?"

"Second in the two hundred metres and second in the four hundred. That's my favourite race." She nods to the back of the room. "Misha Li came first in both, but if I train hard, maybe I can beat her. I'm *passionate* about running."

"I love it too," Jamie says. Telling the truth makes her heart feel as weightless as a helium balloon. "I got fifth in the four hundred at my old school. Uh… maybe we can practise sometime."

Beth's eyes sparkle. "That would be fantastic."

The trio gets busy on their year-end social studies project. Raina sketches her first map.

Beth says, "Jamie, I can finish your research if you want to start on the writing."

"My research is done. But thanks." Jamie hunches over her laptop and notebook, desperate for inspiration. *Why did I say I like writing? I'm never gonna get this done.*

Finally it's nutrition break. Mr. Pratter tells everyone to take their snacks outside.

Jamie nibbles her banana bread as she follows Beth and Raina up the hill to the tall swings surrounded by birch trees. Only two swings are free, so Jamie offers to push both girls. She gobbles the rest of her snack and wipes the crumbs on her shorts. Then she pushes Raina with her right hand and Beth with her left.

At the sound of the bell, Beth jumps off as she's swinging forward and dashes to the field for running practice.

"I guess we better go," says Raina.

The teachers mix the grades into teams. Softball isn't Jamie's favourite sport, but she's glad to be outdoors. And as long as she even bunts the ball, she can usually make it to first base. While she's waiting for her turn at bat, a couple of grade 6 girls ask her name and where she used to live.

"Okay, Jamie, you're up," calls Mr. Pratter.

She grabs an aluminum bat and takes her position at home plate. One runner's on first.

"Hey, my turn to pitch," shouts Jeremy, jogging in from second base. The pitcher tosses him the ball. Jeremy faces Jamie, giving her a beady-eyed look.

Uh-oh. She gulps. *Stuck in his orbit now. The sooner I hit the ball, the sooner I can escape.*

"This should be an easy out," Jeremy mutters, quietly enough so the teachers can't hear him. He throws the pitch.

Jamie swings hard. And totally misses.

"You can do it, Jamie," cheers her teacher.

"Hit it, Jamie," Raina calls.

With the next pitch, Jamie considers taking a big swing but sees the arc is coming up short. Instead, she pushes her bat forward and down. It connects for a bunt.

She drops the bat and sprints, reaching first base before the ball. Safe.

"Woo-hoo!" shouts Raina.

Jamie grins.

The grade 5 boy on first base taunts Jeremy. "Way to go, letting a girl get on base with a bunt."

Jeremy scowls at Jamie. Now she's determined to get more than a base hit when she's up next.

The player ahead of her gets tagged out running to home plate, but Jamie makes it to second. On the next hit she's quick enough to pass third and score a run.

Jeremy's still pitching when Jamie's up to bat again. When he strikes her out, he looks like he wants to do a happy dance. Jamie's face burns with shame as she walks back to her team.

The third time Jeremy pitches to Jamie, he narrows his dark blue eyes again. She hits a grounder past third base and tears off, getting to second base.

Jamie's team ends up winning the game. Jeremy glares at her, then slams his glove to the dirt. She flinches.

"My class, go get your lunches," Mr. Pratter says. "Jamie, hold on a minute."

Her heart rate speeds up. *What did I do?*

"Don't look so worried. Your running is impressive. I want you to race against Misha and Beth after school."

"Oh, uh, okay." *Now I can really be Beth's twin.*

Beth gets to the lunchroom late.

"Jamie was awesome running the bases," Raina says. "She helped us win the game."

"That's tremendous, Jamie. I play Youth Ball. You could sign up next year."

"I'll do that." Jamie drinks from her water bottle, then tells her about the after-school race.

"Weird. We had a practice already," Beth says. "Any idea why?"

"Nope." *But I'm sure pumped he said my running is impressive.*

At dismissal, Jamie follows Beth, Misha and Mr. Pratter to the field. He says, "Girls, you'll run the four hundred metres. Go behind the softball diamond and along the edge of the field, around the playground and back here."

They line up. He says, "On your mark. Get set. GO."

Jamie charges off with the others. Misha's in the lead, her straight black hair whipping around, then Beth, ponytail swishing.

Mr. Pratter shouts across the field, "Push harder."

Jamie's legs itch to run faster, so she picks up her pace. *I'm running as smooth as…as…as peanut butter.* Jamie pulls ahead of Beth.

As Jamie rounds the playground, all she can think of is catching up to Misha. Her leg muscles respond. She passes Misha and blasts by Mr. Pratter first. By several seconds. *Wow.*

Beth, panting, says, "I guess…you do…love running."

"Yeah." Jamie bends at the waist, catching her breath.

"Well done, Jamie," says their teacher. "That qualifies you for the two hundred and four hundred at the district meet. Welcome to the Jaguars."

I get to race at the next level? "Uh…thank you."

Misha pats Jamie on the back. "Good race." Her dark eyes glisten.

"Thanks."

Beaming, Jamie walks toward the school to pick up her backpack. She turns to talk to Beth, but Beth's at the street, already heading home.

Jamie texts Liisa the exciting news. Her reply: **Cool. My fashion design poster won first in the contest!**

No surprise. **Awesome**

When Jamie tells her family about the race at dinner, they whoop for her.

Mom asks, "Who else from your class is going?"

"Misha, Beth—" Jamie's fork slips from her fingers and clangs onto her plate. "Oh no."

Dad eyes her. "What's wrong?"

"Only first and second place at school get to compete."

Jamie's stomach curdles, like how milk reacts when she adds lemon juice for muffin batter. "Beth was supposed to run the two hundred and four hundred, but I stole her spots."

That's why Beth didn't say goodbye after the race. *Ugh—she must be SO mad at me. My Make-a-Friend project is ruined.* "I can't go."

She's relieved that Mom and Dad understand her decision.

Jamie has a restless night, and when morning finally comes she leaves early for school. Mr. Pratter's in the classroom alone when she gets there.

"Hello, Jamie."

"Uh, hi, I…uh, I need to…" Her fingers tremble as she fidgets with a button on her shirt.

"What is it, Jamie?"

"I…I'm not going to the district meet."

"Whyever not?" Mr. Pratter lowers his eyebrows. "You earned the spot and you could win."

"I…I'm…sorry. I can't do it."

Jamie sets her backpack down by her desk, then waits for Beth in the hallway.

When Beth arrives with Raina and sees Jamie, her face freezes with her mouth in a straight line. She zips to her seat without saying a word to anyone.

"Beth," Jamie says, standing in front of her. "I can't go to the meet."

"Are you serious?" Beth's eyes widen, looking hopeful.

"Yeah. Now you can race."

Progress in the Make-a-Friend project.

The social studies project is moving along too. Raina's already drawn both posters. As Jamie starts the written part, she feels nauseous. *Am I coming down with something?* She sneaks her hand up to feel her forehead. Warm. Normal warm.

That evening, Jamie spends more time sharpening her pencil than writing. The girls' research is excellent, especially Beth's, so there's no shortage

28

of information. But Jamie can't think of an original way to write about any of the points.

CHAPTER FIVE

When Jamie arrives at school the next day, Beth is colouring one of the map posters with Raina and looks up. "Hi, Jamie. How's the writing?"

"It's coming." *Slowly. Painfully.*

Raina unrolls her other poster. "This one's done."

"Wow." Raina's obvious talent—and speed—makes Jamie's panic skyrocket. She'll have to work extra hard tonight to get her part done. If only this group project had been in science.

From the moment she gets in the door after school, Jamie attacks the project. She struggles but finally gets through the research and has the required length. It would look better typed, but Beth insisted on seeing it written first.

In the morning, Jamie rechecks her work and her heart plummets. If only she'd never lied. *Should I leave it at home and say I forgot it? No—best get it over with.*

Beth and Raina are in the classroom when Jamie arrives. She fishes the project out of her backpack.

Beth stands and snatches the papers. "I can't wait to read it." She scans the first page, flips to the next, then quickly to the end, looking horrified. "Seriously? You didn't put much effort into this. I thought you liked writing."

"Let me see." Raina reaches for the work and reads a bit on each page. "Oh."

Beth crosses her arms. "I did more advanced writing than this in grade three. Why'd you—?"

"I'm really sorry," Jamie blurts. Her stomach clenches. "I'm not great at writing, and that's the truth. I'm better at math."

"Well, there's no math in this project." Beth's face is flushed as she grabs the papers and slams them on her desk. "I should've done the writing to start with. Now I have to do the entire project. Thanks a lot." She sits down, adjusts her glasses and starts madly scribbling.

Meanwhile Raina spreads out her map. She opens her pencil case, selects a dark shade of green and fills in birch leaves.

Jamie whispers, "I could help colour."

Raina says nothing and angles her body away.

Beth and Raina huddle together during nutrition and activity breaks.

There's no invitation to sit with them at lunch.

They ignore her all afternoon.

Jamie walks home alone and gags on the clump of sadness stuck in her throat. She blew it. Back to no friends. She doesn't even want to text Liisa. Jamie hasn't heard from her in days. *She probably doesn't care about me anymore.*

Summer stretches ahead of Jamie like a desolate moonscape. If only her family had never moved here. *How will I spend my friendless summer?*

Out of habit, Jamie starts up the family computer to check what scientists have seen with NASA's space telescope. What if they find an Earth-sized planet that's livable? Jamie puzzles over the universe for the thousandth time, picturing galaxies after galaxies of stars, going on forever. Thinking about NASA's search for new things speeds her pulse. Exploring. Discovery. Adventure.

Their missions are more exciting than a model boat travelling Paddle's route, but Jamie's idea would still be an adventure. Especially if she can track the boat somehow. Maybe she *could* build that model after all.

Why not? No one cares what I do anyway.

Jamie shuffles to her bedroom where her models wait for her like old friends. She's proud of them, but they have no moving parts. No usefulness. All they do is sit on her dresser.

I want to make a model that actually does *something*.

All through supper, questions about Paddle's adventure bubble up in Jamie. Finally Brock's in bed, Mom's curled up with a novel and Dad's settled into his recliner with a crossword puzzle. "Dad, where did Paddle start out? What creek could take a model boat into the Nipigon River?"

"I don't know." He taps his pen against the page. "A group of stars. Eight letters. Hmm…*cluster*'s too short."

"I know that one, Dad. It's *asterism*."

"Oh, right. Thanks." He fills in the boxes.

"Dad? My creek question?"

"Check the book, and then find a map online." He buries his nose in his puzzle again.

Jamie pulls *Paddle-to-the-Sea* off her shelf and hunts for the map inside. She flips forward and back. Too far, as now she's staring at the copyright page. It was first published in 1941. *Wow*. Jamie does the math. *Double wow. This book is older than Grandpa.*

On the computer, Jamie finds a detailed map of the area. She wants her model boat to follow Paddle's route, but if she launches it that far north, it could get wrecked in one of the hydro dams on the Nipigon River. She locates a creek south of the dams, not far from a road, and follows where it flows. *Yes.* Into the Nipigon River like Paddle's journey. From there the boat would head toward the bridge, slip underneath and float on into Lake Superior.

Jamie gives a quick nod. "*That's* what I'm going to do."

Mom lowers her book. "What are you going to do?"

"Make a model boat, launch it in a creek and track it to see where it goes." That will make the summer fly by. She fizzes with the excitement of starting a new project.

"Great idea," Mom says. "You'll need to use strong materials though."

Dad asks without looking up, "Do you want any help with the design?"

"I'm okay."

Jamie plants herself at the computer desk with a pencil, eraser and pad of paper. She doodles as she thinks about what shape and size are best.

After crumpling several drawings, Jamie sighs so hard, her lips flutter.

Time to go online.

She researches model boat designs. The first model is way too large—almost a metre long. The next one isn't made to go in water, only to be mounted on a stand. Another model is too flimsy. Another has no closed space to protect the equipment she'll need for tracking. *All* of them are too easily broken.

Jamie can't help picturing Niagara Falls. She shudders, imagining her boat tumbling over the edge. She folds her arms. *It's almost as hard to find a design as it is to make a friend.*

She grabs a Granny Smith apple from the bowl on the kitchen table. Taking a huge bite, she clomps to her room. The sour juice totally matches her mood. Jamie glares at her lunar lander. So many times while building it she'd wanted to give up. But it was such a thrill to put the last piece in place.

There *has* to be a way to put together a boat.

Do I even want to do this? She hasn't built a model since the lunar lander. Jamie gently bumps her fingertip down its ladder. She had fun making it, and then Liisa arrived. Liisa had zero interest in math or science or building models. Jamie was so desperate to have a friend, she gave up everything she loved. She convinced herself she'd never build another model.

Liisa only liked me because I made myself her twin. Same with Beth. Until I got caught lying. Jamie chokes back a sob.

After a few deep breaths, she straightens her spine. *Might as well have fun on my own. But there's no way I'm going to tell* anyone *at school about this.*

Jamie rushes back to the living room to use the computer again.

"I thought you'd gone to bed," Dad says. "Off you go."

"Aw, Daaaaaad. I need to figure out my boat."

"You'll think better with a full night's sleep."

Jamie lies awake in bed for ages pondering designs.

CHAPTER SIX

When Jamie wakes up Saturday morning, Mom's on the computer checking her email.

Jamie hovers, still in her pyjamas. "Can you do that on your phone?"

"I only need a few more minutes," Mom says. "Grab some cereal."

Finally Jamie gets her turn. She checks out more and more designs. But none of them are what she needs. *How can it be so tough?*

Brock swoops his toy floatplane beside Jamie's head.

"Fly that somewhere else. I'm doing research here."

The next model she finds uses a solar panel. That might be useful.

But the design is totally wrong.

Dad ambles over, sipping his steaming coffee. "Have you picked something?"

"I can't find a single one that would work."

"What websites did you check?"

"Tons," Jamie barks. She softens her voice. "Sorry, I'm stumped. Maybe this is a bad idea." Tears well in her eyes.

Dad wraps his arm around her shoulders, giving them a squeeze.

Brock zooms his toy powerboat along the floor into the living room. He's pressing down so hard his boat leaves a groove in the carpet.

Jamie gasps. "What if I use Brock's plastic boat? It's strong."

Dad squeezes her shoulders again. "It's worth a try."

"Brock, do you want your boat to travel to the ocean like Paddle, but for real?"

"I dunno." He slides his hand along the hull. "What if it gets stuck in a log like Paddle did? It could get chopped in half."

"Anything could happen, but your boat would have a big adventure." *Us too.*

Brock clasps his boat to his chest. "It's my fav'rite toy."

Only because you saw boats on the screen. "What if I take all your turns to empty the dishwasher for a whole month?"

"Well…"

"Your birthday's coming up. You could ask Grandma and Grandpa to get you a different boat. A pirate ship, maybe."

A broad smile makes his face glow. "Aye aye, matey." He gives the powerboat to Jamie.

"Thanks, Brock." Jamie's lungs feel two sizes larger, breathing more easily knowing she doesn't have to build a boat.

"No dishes for a month! *Aaaaaarrrrrrrrrr!*" He tears away toward his bedroom.

Jamie checks how much space is inside the boat. "Uncle Doug knows about tracking equipment, right, Dad? And if I should use a solar panel to power the batteries?" Uncle Doug's the techiest person Jamie knows.

"Give him a call."

Jamie phones him and explains her project.

"You're right, solar is best," Uncle Doug says. "You'll need high-powered batteries for the GPS. I'll come over tonight and we can brainstorm."

The rest of the morning slug-slithers along. Even

when Mom shoos Jamie outside to ride her bike, she daydreams about making Paddle's journey real. After lunch she reads online about mini solar panels and lightweight, high-powered batteries and tiny GPS units. Her list of questions grows.

After supper Jamie takes Brock's turn unloading the dishwasher. Dad loads it again.

Finally Uncle Doug arrives. Dad and his brother could pass for twins. What's weird is Uncle Doug is younger but has less hair.

Jamie shows him Brock's boat.

He examines it all over. "It's definitely sturdy." This puts a grin on Brock's face.

"So I need a solar panel," says Jamie, "high-powered batteries and a GPS. But how will the GPS send a signal for tracking?"

"It needs a transmitter with an antenna."

"Okay," says Jamie as she writes that on her pad of paper. "Do I use lithium batteries or alkaline batteries? I read that lithium ones last a lot longer, so I think those are better."

"I agree."

"Some won't work below minus twenty."

"Yes, you need to consider that. Great job researching, Jamie."

"Thanks."

They head to the computer and search for items online, discuss options and make their choices.

"Is there room in the boat for everything?"

"I'm fairly sure, but we'll have a better idea once we look at all of it. Monday I'm going to Thunder Bay. I'll pick up everything then."

Jamie races to her bedroom to find her glow-in-the-dark moon bank. Brock says, "Whoa" as she empties it onto the coffee table.

After counting the bills and coins, she asks, "Will fifty-three dollars and forty cents pay for all of it?"

"Not quite."

Brock dashes out of the living room.

Uncle Doug scoops up the money. "But I like your project, so I'll cover the rest." He holds out his right hand. "Deal?"

Jamie firmly shakes his hand. "Deal."

Brock runs back, clutching his yellow race car bank. "Here, Jamie. You can have all my money for your boat."

"Really? Thanks, Brock." Jamie hugs him, then cups her hands to catch the coins as he dumps them out.

Dad tousles Brock's hair. "That's my man."

Uncle Doug hefts the toy boat in one hand. "One more thing. Your boat needs ballast, something to make it heavier along the keel so it's stable in rough waters."

"Sometimes people use stick-on weights in model derby cars to make them heavier," Jamie says, "so they race faster. Would those work?"

"They sure would."

"But I probably have to order them online, and that could take a while." She pauses. "I know something better. I helped Dad fasten wheel weights on the truck tires to balance them. What do you think?"

"Brilliant. You can take care of getting those." He tilts his head toward Brock. "And I'm guessing your brother's money will be enough to pay for them."

Jamie giggles when Brock punches the air, yelling, "Yes!"

CHAPTER SEVEN

At school on Monday morning, Jamie is invisible. Not even her teacher says hello. Although it's a warm day, she shivers. *Did Beth tell him what happened with the project?*

After announcements, Mr. Pratter says, "Everybody, share one thing you're excited about doing in the summer."

Shoot. Jamie should have *known* he'd ask every teacher's favourite end-of-year question. She will not say a word about the trackable boat. But what *can* she say?

"Four-wheeling with our new quad," Jeremy boasts at the front of the classroom.

"Sounds great. Next?"

A girl behind Jamie calls, "I'm excited about going to hockey school."

Noah Danio, longish black hair poking out the sides of his black hoodie and skin darker than Raina's, says, "Fishing with my big brother."

Raina, looking at Noah, says, "Powwow."

"Visiting my cousins in Calgary," mumbles Beth.

"Lots of fun ahead," Mr. Pratter says. "How about you, Jamie?"

She shrugs. Everyone will laugh at her plans.

Mr. Pratter gently says, "It doesn't have to be major."

Jamie shuts her eyes. No one's plans are anything like hers. *Should I think of something different?* But she's only excited about one thing. *What's stopping me? I'm not going to make a friend here anyway.*

Jamie opens her eyes and stares straight ahead, wiping her clammy hands on her shorts. "Launching and tracking my model boat."

Luckily no one laughs. But the classroom's as silent as space. Jamie senses everyone is staring at her. She's an insect under a microscope.

"That sounds interesting," says Mr. Pratter. "What gave you that idea?"

"Uh…*Paddle-to-the-Sea*. The book. I…want to see if my boat follows the same route."

Jeremy twists around to scowl at her. Then he makes a thumbs-down like he's squashing a bug.

Jamie slouches in her seat. All she can think about is bolting out the door. Heat creeps up her neck and floods her face. It takes every shred of willpower for her to stay in her chair.

"I think there's a film version," says Mr. Pratter. "I'll try to find that for us to watch. Next?"

Jamie leans over her desk, forehead on folded arms. Someone taps her lightly on her shoulder.

She peeks—it's Raina, stretching across Beth's desk.

"Building stuff is cool," Raina whispers. "Can I help?"

Jamie's dumbstruck. That Raina would talk to her. That she likes building things. That she wants to help.

Raina's gaze narrows. "If you're telling the truth."

"I *am* launching and tracking a boat. Really," says Jamie. Beth is glaring at her.

"So can I help you?" asks Raina.

Jamie's throat squeezes. "Yeah," she croaks as she bobs her head.

The rest of the morning is a blur. Miraculously Beth completed the writing for the social studies project over the weekend. Jamie's relieved to see her name printed on the cover. Before Beth hands it in, Jamie apologizes again.

Beth harrumphs. "Mr. Pratter needs to be informed."

"Just leave it." Raina holds up her hand, palm facing Beth. "Jamie did her part of the research and she's sorry."

When it's time for lunch, Beth links her arm in Raina's and pulls her ahead, away from Jamie. Jealousy sparks inside her like metal in a microwave.

But in the lunchroom, Raina motions for Jamie to join her and Beth. She holds her egg salad sandwich toward Jamie. "As long as you have something different, I'll take it."

Yuck. "You sure? It's liver sausage."

"It's *got* to be better than this slimy stuff."

"Definitely."

"Or was your 'I love egg salad' a lie too?" Raina chuckles while Beth rolls her eyes.

Wishing she had never fibbed, Jamie's insides squirm. "Guilty. I don't like it, but I'll still trade, if you want."

"You don't have to."

"It's okay." They swap.

As Jeremy passes their table, he elbows Jamie in the back. "Good luck tracking your model boat. You'll lose it the first day."

The meanness in his voice stuns her. The boys with him crack up.

"Get lost, jerk," says Raina. She turns to Jamie. "Ignore him."

Her advice is soothing. Jamie focuses on eating and listening, trying to get to know these two girls. Beth never looks at her. Jamie totally understands. She doubts there's any way to win Beth's friendship.

Leaving school, Raina asks, "Can I come see your model?"

"Sure." *Will she think using Brock's toy boat is dumb?*

Raina whips out her cell phone. "I'll text my mom."

Then a thought strikes Jamie. Her mouth is so dry she has to mega-swallow before she can speak. "Beth, do you want to come too?"

Beth shakes her head and marches off.

47

Raina cups one hand around her mouth. "She's still super mad at you. Besides, she hates everything to do with making models, and science and math. You know, all the fun stuff."

Despite feeling awful about deceiving Beth and Raina, Jamie can't help grinning. "I never thought this would happen."

"What?"

"Meeting another girl who likes building stuff."

"Yup, machines, models, beaded medallions. Ever since I built a 3-D puzzle I've loved making things." Raina walks as quickly as she talks. "My first model was a simple wooden Ferris wheel from a kit—boring. Then a couple more complicated kits. Now I design my own projects and shop for parts. I even built a Rube Goldberg machine."

"Wow—those are complicated. I've made three models—with help," Jamie admits. "And I always give my dad a hand with building projects."

"Same here."

"I need to buy some wheel weights," Jamie says, "for ballast."

"Ooh, I love it. Can I look for those with you?"

"Sure."

"Canadian Tire isn't far." Raina points ahead.

"Let's go there first."

"Okay. I like how close everything is in this town." Jamie texts her mom to tell her the plan.

The store sign calls it the smallest Canadian Tire in Canada. Raina zips past the camping supplies and sporting goods, directly to the automotive section. The girls search the aisles.

"Look." Jamie holds up a package of steel weights. "It says these ones have adhesive. You just peel off the backing."

"Stick-ons are better than clip-ons for this project."

"Great, I'll get these." Jamie lines up at the cashier.

Raina joins her. "Anything else you need for building your boat? Glue? Screws? Or some—"

"I'm…" whispers Jamie, hoping Raina will lower her voice. "I'm not actually *building* the boat." She hands the wheel weights to the cashier.

Raina grabs Jamie's wrist. "What do you mean, 'not building' it?"

Jamie faces her. "I—I researched different designs and none of them would last long in water. Then I…" Taking a big breath, she continues, "I decided my brother's toy boat would be a better choice."

"Oh." Raina's eyebrows scrunch together and her shoulders slump.

She *does* think it's a dumb idea.

The cashier tells Jamie how much she owes.

"So," Raina says in a low, dull voice, "you don't need help building anything."

Say something or she'll leave. Jamie gulps.

"You lied again. I'm going home." Raina walks toward the door.

Jamie can't find the words she needs. It's all over. *I knew it wouldn't last. Failed again.* By the time she pays for the weights, Raina has left the store.

CHAPTER EIGHT

Jamie sprints outside. Raina's up ahead. How can Jamie convince her to stay involved? She doubts anything will work.

But the worst already happened, didn't it?

"Raina, wait."

Raina keeps walking.

"Please stop." Jamie runs after her. "I never said I was building one, just launching and tracking."

Raina pivots. "But when I asked if I could help you *build* it, why didn't you tell me you weren't?"

Tears brim in Jamie's eyes. "I was so excited you wanted to help." *And be my friend.* "I'm sorry."

Raina doesn't move.

"You can help fit the tracking equipment in the boat." Jamie wipes her eyes with the back of her hand.

Raina gazes past her.

"And test it. And launch the boat with us."

No response.

Jamie's pulse accelerates. "Raina, I really want you to be part of this. Please say yes."

Raina looks down and tucks a loose strand of hair behind her ear. "Building *is* the best, but... getting the tracking to work could be fun." A flicker of a smile crosses her face. "Okay. I'm in."

Jamie exhales. "Great."

When they reach Jamie's house, they find Mom in the living room. Her painting of Lake Superior is propped against the couch, ready to hang.

"Hi, Mom, this is Raina." Jamie nods toward the painting. "Wow, it looks just like the photo."

Mom stops hammering a nail in the wall and looks over her shoulder. "Thanks, sweetie. Hi, Raina."

Mom winks at Jamie, making her cringe. *Hope Raina didn't notice.*

Thankfully Raina is studying Mom's painting. "Hi. Amazing waves."

"Thank you, how kind. I love doing waterscapes. How was your day, Jamie?"

"Okay. Raina wants to see the boat."

"Wonderful. It's an interesting project."

Once they're in Jamie's bedroom, Raina inspects her three models. "Good job."

"Thanks." Jamie glows.

Looking at the bookshelf, Raina selects the book about Leonardo da Vinci's inventions. "Hey, can I borrow this?"

"Sure." Jamie offers her the book of science experiment challenges. "Have you seen this one?"

Raina checks out a few pages. "Can I—?"

"Yeah, take it too."

"You've got a Barbie?" Raina lifts the pristine Barbie from the lowest shelf, still in its unopened package. She laughs. "You like dolls as much as I do."

"I've had it since I was five. I only keep it because my Nana gave it to me."

"It doesn't matter who gives them to me," Raina says. "They go straight to the thrift store."

Jamie hands Raina the toy powerboat. "Here it is."

She examines it bow to stern. "This *is* super strong. It'll work really well."

"Let's see if the wheel weights fit inside." Jamie unwraps the package and carefully breaks one off the strip so the backing stays on. She hands it to Raina.

Raina slides the weight inside the boat, placing it on the bottom. "Perfect size. You—uh—*we* can fit all of them inside if we need to."

Jamie adds, "We should wait until we've sorted out the tracking equipment before we fasten any."

Raina removes the weight. "And we can test-float the boat to figure out how many weights it needs."

Jamie's phone rings. "It's my uncle—he's helping with the equipment," she tells Raina before answering the call. "Hi, Uncle Doug. We found the wheel weights. Did you get all the other equipment?"

"I bought everything except the transmitter," Uncle Doug says. "It's out of stock right now. No idea when it will be available."

"Oh." Jamie's heart sinks as she exhales.

Raina raises both hands, palms up, mouthing, "What?"

"Would another store have a transmitter?" Jamie asks.

Raina nods, then says loud enough for Uncle Doug to hear, "Or can we get it online?"

"That's Raina." Jamie holds the phone so they can both listen. "She's helping with the project."

"Nice," Uncle Doug replies. "Can you two search online?"

Raina smiles and Jamie says, "No problem."

"If you find one, I'll order it when I get back."

"Thank you." Jamie scurries to the computer to explore sites selling transmitters.

"What's your Wi-Fi password?" Raina asks. "I'll search on my phone." Jamie enters the password.

Eventually Raina finds a transmitter that's right for the boat. "And it's in stock."

Jamie peers at Raina's screen. "How long will it take to come?"

Raina taps "Buy Now" to find out. "Two days, but that's to a city, so make it three."

Jamie lets out a happy shriek. "We should have it by Friday."

"Hey, this was fun," Raina says, glancing at the time on her phone, "but I better get going. Meet me and Beth at the end of your street—at eight forty-five—to walk to school, okay?"

"I'll be there." Jamie waits until Raina is striding down the side of the road before she hops a few times and cheers.

CHAPTER NINE

In the morning, Jamie hurries through breakfast. She dashes to the meeting spot a few minutes early.

Raina and Beth round the corner chatting so intently they don't see Jamie until they're about ten steps away.

"Hi-Raina-hi-Beth," Jamie says, speaking so quickly her words blend together. She inhales a deep breath to calm down.

Beth gives Jamie a hard look.

"Hey, Jamie." Raina waves. "Did your uncle order the transmitter?"

"Yeah." As they walk, Jamie fills them in on the plan to install and test the equipment Saturday morning.

Raina whoops.

"Can you come over at ten o'clock?"

"Yup."

Beth grabs Raina's upper arm. "But you're coming to the pancake breakfast with me and Mom."

"I can still do that *and* be at Jamie's at ten."

Beth frowns. "I don't want to rush."

Jamie guesses Beth is hoping to have Raina to herself for longer than breakfast. "I'll ask my uncle if he can come in the afternoon instead."

Beth's frown shrinks a bit. "Thanks."

During lunch, Beth monopolizes Raina. So Jamie takes out her phone and looks up female Canadian astronauts.

Dr. Jenni Sidey-Gibbons catches her eye. She's an engineer and combustion scientist, part of the Lunar Gateway project that will help to set up a research centre on the moon. *Cool—what if the first Canadian on the moon is a woman?*

Jamie keeps reading. Dr. Sidey-Gibbons helped organize a chapter of Robogals at her university.

What's that?

The article says Robogals tries to get more girls and young women involved in STEM—science, technology, engineering and mathematics. Jamie finds their website. Free workshops for girls...

building robots and learning computer programming…chapters at Canadian universities…

Sign me up!

She taps the Find a Chapter button. *Shoot.* The nearest one is in southern Ontario. Thunder Bay has Lakehead University, where Dad studied. *Why doesn't LU have one?* On the LU website, Jamie learns they teach engineering. Back at Robogals, she sees a box with the words, "No chapter? Let us know."

Should I? Eeeek!

She taps Contact Your Region and sends a message asking what she needs to do to start a chapter.

The end-of-break bell startles Jamie, and she realizes Beth and Raina have left.

She pockets her phone and heads to her classroom. For absolutely sure she's not going to tell anyone about Robogals in case nothing happens. She doesn't want people thinking she's a liar anymore.

Even math problems don't keep Jamie's mind off Robogals. It sounds more exciting than the game-coding workshop Jamie took last year. There are so many things she'd program a robot to do.

Number one: emptying the dishwasher. She's sick of doing every load herself. Then again, she *does* have Brock's boat in exchange.

Mr. Pratter ends the dismissal announcements by telling the students going to the district track and field meet the next day what they need to bring. "The bus is leaving *before* school starts, at eight forty-five a.m. sharp. If you're late, you'll miss out."

"Good luck, Beth," says Jamie. "I hope you win." That gets a hint of a smile from her.

On the way to school on Thursday, Beth talks nonstop about the district meet. "We had SO much fun. The four hundred was the last event. I felt exhausted at the start, but somehow I got this spurt of energy and actually passed Misha. I couldn't believe it. She came third and I came second. *And* I got a personal best of one minute, fourteen-point-six-nine seconds."

Raina gives Beth a sideways hug. "You're amazing!"

"Good for you," says Jamie, but Beth doesn't even look her way.

"How'd Noah do in long jump?" asks Raina.

"Ooh, and why are *you* so curious?" says Beth, wiggling her pale eyebrows. "He got second."

"Woo-hoo!" cries Raina.

After school, when the three girls reach Jamie's street on their way home, Raina invites her over to see her models.

"Definitely. I'll drop off my backpack at home and let my mom know."

"I'll come with you."

Beth says, "Nerd time. See you."

The nerds exchange grins. For the first time in her life, Jamie feels okay being called a nerd.

Raina says, "Beth, you're missing out on a great time."

Scrunching her nose, Beth makes it clear she couldn't disagree more. Jamie stifles a giggle.

At home, Mom's face lights up when Jamie tells her the plan. "Wonderful—have fun."

Heading to Raina's, Jamie feels like someone else—a normal girl hanging out with a friend. She's as light as an astronaut bounding on the moon.

When they walk into Raina's room, Jamie gasps at the sight of her models. "I *love* your Space Shuttle."

"I knew that would be your favourite."

"Nice metal bridge. Is it your own design?"

"Yup."

In a high-pitched voice, Jamie says, "Aw, cute Ferris wheel."

"Painted it. All. By. My. Self." Raina talks like a kindergartener.

Jamie stares at the intricate beading project partway finished on Raina's desk. "This is incredible." The flower sewn on felt has hundreds of tiny pink beads crammed together. "You designed this?"

"Uh-huh. A wild rose medallion." Raina caresses a completed petal. "Nokomis—my grandma—says she's never seen anyone learn to bead so fast or so young."

"I thought *I* had patience, but you win."

"Thanks."

"What was the hardest part of building the shuttle?"

"Some pieces were super tiny. Not as small as those beads, but still." Raina opens a binder and flips to the instruction sheet for the shuttle. She recounts the challenges as Jamie reads along.

When Raina's mom says it's suppertime and invites Jamie to stay, she's stunned it's so late. All that time with Raina seemed like only half an hour.

After their burger supper, Jamie heads home and opens her email. She's surprised to see a message from Robogals.

"We're delighted you want to join our team," it starts. *Oh.* They want to know the name of her university and if she's an undergraduate or graduate student. So only a university student can start a chapter? *Darn.*

Wait a minute—there must be another way. Jamie types her reply: "I am a gr 4 girl. I want Robogals at Lakehead U in Thunder Bay. How do I do that?"

CHAPTER TEN

Midmorning the next day, Jamie and Raina sit sideways on their chairs, talking quietly behind Beth about their Saturday plans.

"Jamie," Mr. Pratter says, "what's so important it can't wait until lunch?"

Her cheeks feel as hot as lava. *Wish he'd asked Raina.* "The trackable boat I, uh, Raina and I are working on. We're installing the equipment tomorrow."

"That's exciting. Bring Raina up here and tell us about your project."

Jamie slowly stands, glancing at Raina, who gives her a reassuring smile. Raina strides to the front and Jamie follows. As they take turns explaining, Jamie gradually relaxes. Her voice grows stronger and steadier.

Beth seems to be paying attention, at least. But no one else besides Mr. Pratter looks interested.

Except maybe—just maybe—Jeremy's scowl is only half-strength.

The teacher says, "Keep us posted."

When they return to their desks, Beth whisper-hisses, "Raina, don't forget we have the pancake breakfast tomorrow."

*
**

Raina is back at Jamie's after school. Having her over feels so natural already. They munch on popcorn and watch YouTube maker videos.

"What should we name our boat?" Jamie feels warm from the inside out saying "our."

"It's a lot like Paddle, so Paddle-to-the-Sea Two?"

"T-w-o or t-o-o?"

Raina laughs. "T-o-o makes it sound like our boat has already reached the sea."

"But it's a power boat, not a paddling one." Brock carries the toy vessel to the girls in the living room. "Look, I helped you."

Jamie lunges, grabbing the boat. Wheel weights decorate the outside. "No! Why'd you do that?"

"I thought I could 'cause my money paid for them." Brock pouts.

Jamie stomps and growls.

"How come you're mad? I did my best counting. I stuck zactly six on each side."

"They're supposed to go on the *inside*," Raina says, "along the bottom. And only as many as we need."

"Oh. Sorry." Brock tries to hug his sister, but Jamie huffs, turning away.

"Apology *not* accepted. You ruined it." She sounds pathetic but doesn't care.

"I gotta go," Raina says.

The back of Jamie's neck feels warm and tingly. *Is she leaving because of me?*

"But I want to know if you can fix it." Raina holds her phone, ready to tap. "What's your number? I'll text you so you have mine."

Jamie exhales in relief and gives her number to Raina.

After Raina leaves, Jamie searches online for tips on how to remove wheel weights.

A video pops up showing how special pliers work to take wheel weights off tire rims. "Bingo." Maybe Dad has a pair.

Brock follows her out to the garage. After Jamie sets down the little boat, she roots through Dad's toolbox and finds the pliers.

Finally she looks at her brother. His eyes are red and swollen.

Good. He SHOULD cry after wrecking my project.

But then Brock squeezes his eyelids shut. Snuffles loudly.

She slides her arm around him. "Come on, buddy, you can help fix your mess."

Jamie shows him how to grip the boat at either end. She grabs the hull and slides the prongs of the pliers around one of the weights. "Have you got a good hold?"

"With all my muscle."

Jamie squeezes the handles together, grabbing the wheel weight with the prongs. But they slip and the weight doesn't budge. She lines up the prongs again, squeezes and rocks the pliers forward. Then back. They never touch the boat, and the weight lifts off.

"Yeah!" She inspects the side of the boat. No marks. "This is tough plastic. Keep holding tight, Brock."

"Okay."

Jamie slides the prongs around the next weight. She rocks the tool and the weight comes free. It doesn't take long to remove them all. She calls Raina. "Good news—they're off and the boat's not wrecked."

"Yay! We can still use them. I'll bring my super-glue tomorrow so we can stick them inside."

"Thanks."

"Hey, my family's going out to our camp on Sunday. Dad promised we can have a bonfire after supper. Wanna come?"

"Camp? Uh, sure."

"Great. I invited Beth too. I want you to be friends. It's gonna be fun."

Jamie hopes with all her heart that Raina's right. But if Beth ignores her the whole time, it'll be anything but fun.

Later, as Jamie rips up lettuce for salad, she tells Mom about Raina's invitation. "I can go, right?"

Mom's knife hovers above the tomato she's about to slice. "You said Sunday, until late?"

"Uh-huh."

"That's Father's Day."

"Oh yeah." Jamie sighs. "You and Dad want me

to have a friend, though, don't you?"

"Of course, Jamie. But it's important to celebrate Dad too." Mom cuts the slices into pieces. "Besides, you'll be spending all afternoon with her tomorrow."

"I was thinking of Beth. She's going too." *Not that she's ever going to be my friend.*

"I suppose we *could* make a special breakfast before you go—"

"Yeah." Jamie quickly nods. "I'll make Finnish pancakes like Liisa's mom taught me. You know, the thin ones?"

"That would be wonderful. I'll see if Dad's okay with this."

At dinner, Jamie thinks her father is even more awesome when he says, "Love the Dad's Day pancake plan. Breakfast is my favourite meal."

On Saturday afternoon, Jamie and Raina work with Uncle Doug. They set out the tracking equipment, wheel weights and superglue on the kitchen table. Brock watches from his Lego construction site in the living room.

"Okay, what's first?" asks Uncle Doug.

68

"I'll start with these." Jamie picks up two weights. "But I won't glue them yet. If we lightly tape the equipment inside, we can test how it floats and then add more weights if we need to."

"Great idea," Uncle Doug says.

Raina pulls a clear plastic bag from her jacket pocket. "We can test-float in this in the kitchen sink."

"Good plan." Jamie tears small pieces of duct tape, tacking them to the glue bottle so they're handy. "Right, we need to research how to water-proof our boat."

"First," Uncle Doug says, "which items must go *inside* the boat?"

"Batteries." Jamie tapes them in place.

"GPS too." Raina sticks on a loop of duct tape and attaches the small device.

Jamie grabs the solar panel. "This needs sun-light, so it goes on the top."

"So does this." Raina holds up the transmitter.

"You two engineers don't even need me," Uncle Doug says.

Jamie gives him a friendly bump with her shoul-der. "You can fill the sink with water."

He laughs and turns on the tap.

Raina spreads open the bag. Jamie places the

boat inside. They hold opposite top edges of the bag and gingerly lower it into the water. The boat leans to one side, then the other.

Jamie squints at the keel. "It's not stable. I'll add four more weights."

Raina lifts the boat from the bag and removes the equipment. Jamie inserts the extra pieces of steel. When they reload and float it again, it looks balanced.

"Three more things," calls Brock, rummaging through the Lego bin. He finds a girl with black hair and brown skin—Raina. And a fair, brown-haired one—Jamie. Then a boy with hair as dark brown as his.

"Thanks." Jamie fist-bumps him.

Raina duct-tapes the Lego kids inside. Their faces peek out from behind the windshield. The boat passes the floating test perfectly.

"Back to waterproofing." Uncle Doug picks up the vessel. "We need to protect this equipment."

Everyone crowds around the computer while Jamie searches online. They compare products to find the toughest waterproof tape.

"With the boat already bright red," Raina says, "I think clear repair tape is best."

Jamie gives a thumbs-up.

Uncle Doug says, "I'll buy some tomorrow."

"This card I made can go on the bow," Jamie says. "After I print the name, I'll get it laminated."

"Let's see." Raina takes Jamie's card that has her name and address and Raina's name. "Should we put your email address too?"

"Right, I'll add it."

Raina then reads aloud, "'Meet *blank*, seeking the ocean. Please help *blank* on its way. Thank you.' We've *got* to think up a name."

"Not my department." Uncle Doug holds up his hands, fingers spread. "Okay, time to test this. The batteries are fully charged."

"Should we take everything out?" Jamie asks.

"Yes. You girls can connect the pieces."

Raina and Jamie carefully remove the equipment, then figure out how to plug the components together. They only need a bit of help.

"That sure was complicated," Jamie says, "but we did it!"

"You two amaze me," Uncle Doug says.

Next, they test it. Incredibly everything works.

"So, this," Raina says, tapping the solar panel, "will charge the batteries that run the GPS, right?

And the transmitter that sends the location?"

"Right," Jamie says. "And, Uncle Doug, the GPS coordinates get to your cell phone through a satellite, right?"

"Correct."

"Awesome," exclaims Raina.

The girls disconnect the equipment. Then they glue the weights and Lego kids in place and install the equipment inside and on the back of the little boat, reconnecting the pieces.

Everything works.

Raina shouts, "We rock!"

"Well done," says Uncle Doug. "Let's test it from my boat on Wednesday night, say six o'clock?"

The girls agree.

"If all goes well, we can launch it next Saturday," exclaims Jamie.

Mom brings out vanilla ice cream with chocolate fudge sauce and cut-up strawberries. While the kids devour their treat in the kitchen, the adults enjoy theirs out on the deck.

Jamie slurps the last of her chocolate-berry-cream. "I'd love to have a website that shows our boat's GPS coordinates. But that's probably hard to do."

"I helped Mr. Pratter make our class website," says Raina. "I'm sure there's a way. Then we can add the URL to the card with the other info."

"Definitely."

The girls stack their dishes in the sink, then search online for how to create a website. They find a tool that claims to be simple to use. The first task is to choose a domain name.

"I think our boat's name should be part of it," says Raina.

"Good idea. We really need to figure that out." Jamie rests her chin in her hand, elbow on the desk. "But who's going to pay for the website?"

"Your parents?"

Jamie and Raina run out to the deck and ask.

Before either parent can answer, Uncle Doug says, "Let me take care of the registration and hosting."

"Thanks so much," says Jamie.

"Tell me as soon as possible what domain name you want."

"I set up my artist website," says Mom, "so I can help you. Decide what you want it to do."

Her offer floods Jamie with relief. "A zoom-in-able map that shows the boat's location."

"Photos," adds Raina.

"And a comments section," says Jamie.

"That didn't take long." Uncle Doug chuckles.

Mom says, "We can start working on it Monday evening."

"Maybe it'll be ready before the launch," says Raina.

The girls happy-dance around the deck.

CHAPTER ELEVEN

Twenty minutes into the drive to Raina's camp, Beth finally stops talking only with Raina and looks at Jamie. "I hear you got your boat functioning."

"Yeah." Jamie's surprised Beth wants to know about it. "It's really fun how—"

"Speaking of boats," Beth says, "Raina, are we going out in yours today?"

"No," says Raina. "Dad has to do some repairs on it. But we can hike up to the cave. That way we'll get hot enough for a swim in the lake."

When they reach the end of the narrow driveway, Raina's dad parks and the girls help carry bags and boxes over to the cabin. Beyond the sandy beach and dock, the huge lake sparkles.

Jamie checks around for more buildings. Besides a shed, there's only a small one with a chimney, closer to the water. Likely a sauna. "Raina, where's the rest of your camp?"

"Huh? What do you mean? This is it," she says, pointing at the cabin.

"Oh, got it. I call this a cottage and you call it a camp."

Raina laughs. "So that's why you sounded so strange when I invited you here."

Jamie gets sweaty on the hike and itchy from dozens of bug bites. That swim in Lake Superior can't come soon enough.

From behind them on the gravel road, a quad roars past super close. The rider makes a U-turn and zooms up to the girls.

"Hey, it's the boat trackers. What's up?" he says. *Jeremy.*

"You know what's up," Raina says. "Your time with us."

Jamie hides her smirk.

Jeremy stands up on the footrests. "Just being friendly. It's what we do at camp."

Away from the other boys, he sounds normal.

Raina folds her arms. "You should pretend school is camp."

Ignoring her, he turns to Jamie. "What kind of

transmitter are you using for your boat?"

Jamie steps back, eyeing him, her mouth as dry as lunar dust.

"What, is it a secret?" he asks.

"No," croaks Jamie. She clears her throat and tells him the brand.

"Huh. Stupid choice."

Jamie gapes. Doubt rushes through her.

He sits down. "Gotta go." The tires whip the loose gravel behind him as he takes off.

"What does *he* know?" Beth says.

Jeremy thinks my project is dumb. Maybe he's just being mean. Uncle Doug picked the transmitter, so Jamie decides not to worry.

The girls get changed in the cabin. They drop their towels on the beach and race into the lake. In a few minutes they're chilled and running out to wrap themselves in their towels.

Beth perches on a sun-warmed rock and doodles in the smooth sand with a stick.

Raina points out into the lake. "I wonder if our boat will travel past here."

"Not if the currents take it west, like with Paddle." Jamie shakes water out of her ears. "We still need to give it a name."

"Too bad Paddle doesn't work," says Raina.

Jamie blots her ponytail with her towel. "What do you think of Scout?"

Raina screws up her mouth. "It's kind of lame."

"Yeah. And Seafarer sounds too fancy." Jamie sighs and wriggles her feet in the fine grains.

Beth draws a wave pattern in the sand.

Jamie swallows. "Beth, can you think of a name for our boat?"

She keeps tracing lines. *Please don't ignore me.*

Then Beth looks up. "Well, it's seeking the sea, so how about Seeker?"

"I like the sound of that," Raina says.

"Beth, I *love* it." Jamie bounces on her toes. "Oh—we could spell it S-e-*a*-k-e-r, as in the sea."

"That's epic," Raina says.

Beth smiles. "It's unique."

The girls high-five all around.

Beth says, "Raina, remember when the Paddle-to-the-Sea Park opened? My grandma was on the committee that got the grant to build it. She was ecstatic."

"She wasn't the only one," Raina says with a grin. "Remember the day our class first went to the park?"

"And Jeremy climbed onto the rocks—" Beth is laughing too hard to talk.

"You should have seen it, Jamie," says Raina. "He fell in the pond and got soaked." Now all three girls are in hysterics.

All through the barbecue supper and joking and s'mores around the bonfire, Jamie can't believe she's having so much fun.

During block 2 on Monday, Jamie and Raina go online and find the website tool. They whisper-chat about the domain name.

"How about seaker dot c-a?" asks Raina.

Jamie types it in. "Voilà, it's available. I'll let my uncle know."

After lunch Mr. Pratter says, "The weather's nice enough to take science outdoors."

Jamie's so curious about what experiment they'll get to do outside, she imagines her ears are pricked like a deer's.

"Bring paper and something to write with."

That's all? Boring.

The class gathers on the lawn.

"We're doing Alien Linguistics from Bob McDonald's book *An Earthling's Guide to Outer Space*. First, pick a partner."

The girls automatically pair up—without Jamie.

Mr. Pratter asks Noah, "Do you still need a partner?"

With eyes lowered and his black hoodie up as usual, Noah says, "Yes." He shoves his hands in his hoodie pocket and his bangs flop over his brown eyes.

"Who else doesn't have a partner?"

Jamie cringes and raises her hand.

"Okay, Noah and Jamie, you're partners."

Jeremy sings, "Oo-ooh, Noah has a girlfriend."

Jamie's sure her face matches Raina's red top.

Raina looks at Noah with a weird expression. *Does she wish she was my partner?*

Mr. Pratter says, "Groups, spread out and whisper so you keep your ideas to yourselves. Design a message to an alien civilization. You're not allowed to use any Earth words, symbols or numbers, so you need to draw to communicate."

Noah motions with his head to an empty spot on the grass. They walk over, and, looking down, he asks, "Can you draw?"

Jamie's so relieved he's not Jeremy, she's hardly shy. "Yeah, I can." *But using numbers would be more fun.*

They sit facing each other.

Noah whispers, "Got any ideas?"

"How about saying, 'We don't want to hurt you, we just want to learn about you'?"

"So maybe a person smiling with hands like this?" Noah holds out his hands, palms up.

"Yeah. Hopefully the aliens think smiling is friendly. We could show another person with their hands around their ears, wanting to listen." Jamie starts drawing.

"Good idea. What if the first one holds out some food?"

"Okay. These should work as long as the aliens know ears hear and food gives energy." Jamie sketches the two people, erasing some bits and redrawing them.

"So," Noah says, leaning over, studying her pictures, "your boat thing?"

"We named it *Seaker*."

"I like it. But why are you doing it?"

"'Cause it's fun and a challenge. I don't know if it can actually be done."

He juts out his chin, nodding like he approves. Jamie curls herself over the paper, hiding her grin.

"All right, time's up. Gather in a circle over here." After the class is settled, Mr. Pratter says, "Who wants to show their message first?"

Jeremy's arm shoots high. He lifts his group's drawing of a stick figure with two fingers up in a V.

Misha raises her tan-coloured arm. "That's easy. We come in peace. And we're really skinny."

Everyone laughs.

After all the groups have shared their drawings, the class heads back inside.

"*You're* sure the lucky one," says Raina, poking Jamie's side. "If *I* had to work with a boy, I'd pick Noah."

"Yeah." Jamie giggles. "He's nice. And he thinks *Seaker* is cool."

"He does?"

"He didn't exactly say 'cool,' but he likes it," says Jamie. Raina smiles and looks over toward Noah.

At home later, Jamie's excited to find a reply from Robogals. She opens the email. "We love your enthusiasm"—Jamie smiles, then reads further—"but the chapter must be initiated by a professor or student." *So I just need to find someone.* Jamie searches the LU website for the name and email address of the person in charge of the engineering department. *Okay, Jamie, you can do this—be brave.* Her fingers type: "Have you ever heard of Robogals? It's a really fun + interesting way to get girls like me in gr. 4 doing more science. Please can you please start a chapter at Lakehead U?" and she clicks Send.

Did I really do that?

CHAPTER TWELVE

Tuesday is the year-end field trip. The students in grades 4 to 8 will hike from school to Doghead Mountain for a cookout. Ms. Evans, the teacher in charge, gives final instructions: "You *must* remain in your group of five with your supervising adult AT ALL TIMES. No exceptions."

Jamie's group has all of the grade 4 girls with Raina's mom, Mrs. Larouche, as their supervisor. The sun is drying the pavement after the overnight storm. As they head off, Jamie searches her backpack. "I'm *sure* I brought my water bottle." But she finds only her jacket and snack bag.

Beth taps Jamie's shoulder. "Someone always forgets, so I bring an extra." She offers a fluorescent green water bottle and laughs. "There's no way you'll lose it. Don't worry, it's hygienic."

"Thanks, Beth."

Their route takes them downhill, through town, onto the walkway of the Nipigon River Bridge, across the highway and along a dirt road. Finally they reach the hiking trail through the forest, where shady parts of the path are a bit muddy. When the students and their supervisors are almost at the peak, they collect fallen branches for the bonfire.

From the top of Doghead Mountain, the hikers can see Lake Helen, the towers of the bridge, all of Nipigon, over to Red Rock and out to Nipigon Bay in Lake Superior. There's not a cloud in sight. The kids who forgot to put on sunscreen already have red noses.

The grade 8 students, with the adults' help, start the bonfire and set out the hot dog supplies. Other groups collect branches for roasting sticks.

Jamie finds two and hurries to rejoin her friends. The trio giggles as they snap twigs and leaves off their sticks. Ms. Evans supervises them as they sharpen the end to a point with pocket knives.

When the fire has burned down to coals, Jamie's grade gets to roast their hot dogs first. *Woo-hoo!* She skewers a hot dog lengthwise on her roasting stick. She's lost too many to the fire putting them on sideways. Holding it over the coals, she watches the meat sizzle. Soon it's done to perfection, smothered with mustard and relish in a bun. *Yum.* Hiking and eating outside—best day of school yet.

Once everyone's finished eating, the oldest students put out the fire. Meanwhile, the other groups start the hike back, with the grade 6 students leading the way. Soon there's a gap between Jamie's group and the boys dawdling behind them.

Misha's being a goofball, zigzagging along the path. Mrs. Larouche calls, "Slow down," but she runs faster.

Then Misha disappears, followed by a scream.

Branches snap. Another scream. Jamie's group rushes to where they last saw Misha. Beyond the path is a muddy slope with bent bushes where she slid down.

"Help!" yells Misha. "I can't climb back up. I keep sliding."

Raina peers over the edge. "I see you, Misha!" She gingerly steps down, gripping a shrub.

Mrs. Larouche orders, "Raina, get back on the path." She pulls out her phone. "I'm calling Ms. Evans."

"I'm okay, Mom." But then Raina's foot slips. Her

mother gasps and lunges, catching Raina's arm to help her scramble back up.

Raina stares at her mucky shoes as she wipes them on moss. "It's too slippery to go down safely."

"We need a rope," says Jamie.

Beth says, "We only have a first aid kit."

"Okay, so what else?" Jamie glances around. "I know! Everyone, give me your jackets."

Mrs. Larouche and the girls shove theirs at her. Jamie knots the sleeve of Mrs. Larouche's jacket to hers and hers to Raina's. Jamie calls, "Misha, we're working on a way to haul you up."

Soon Jamie's tied five jackets together.

Mr. Pratter and his group of boys arrive. Huffing, the teacher says, "We heard screams. What happened?"

As Raina's mom explains, Jeremy gets the boys to dig their jackets out of their backpacks. He passes them one at a time to Mr. Pratter, who attaches them to the jacket-rope. Then he tests Jamie's knots to make sure they're tight. "All good. Nice secure knots."

Jamie moves to the edge of the path and throws the end of the jacket-rope down to Misha. It lands out of her reach.

"Here, Jamie, put this rock in the sleeve and tie knots around it," says Jeremy. "That'll give you better control."

Wow—he actually sounds friendly.

Jeremy plunks the rock in her hand. She secures it in place in the end sleeve while another group of students appears on the trail.

This time Jamie's trajectory is accurate, with the rock falling just past Misha but where she's able to reach the jacket-rope.

"Tie the first jacket around your waist," calls Jamie. "A double knot as tight as you can. We'll pull you up."

"No, stop," says Mrs. Larouche. "Ms. Evans said not to try rescuing her until she gets here."

"Okay," says Jamie, "but we need more jackets attached so people can pull."

Mr. Pratter secures the ones from the new group.

Ms. Evans arrives and peers down the slope. "Misha? Are you injured?"

"No, I'm fine, just stuck."

As Ms. Evans eyes the jacket-rope, Mr. Pratter assures her he checked every knot or tied it himself.

"Misha, I'm coming down to help you up," calls Ms. Evans. Even though she's wearing hiking boots, it looks like Ms. Evans is having a hard time staying upright as she descends alongside the rope, checking each knot.

A few minutes later, she shouts, "Misha's ready."

Mr. Pratter anchors the end jacket around his waist like in a tug-of-war match. The adults and biggest students grip the jacket-rope.

"Okay, everyone," calls Mr. Pratter, "on the count of three, pull. One, two, *three*."

Muscles tense, arms haul, jackets strain. Thankfully not a single one rips.

"Ouch…*aack*…ooh," exclaims Misha, slipping a few times on her way up. She emerges from the bushes, hair full of dead leaves. Her face is scratched and flushed, her clothes and runners muddy. As she's sitting on the path panting, Ms. Evans scrabbles up behind her.

Misha brushes twigs off her shirt. "Thank you, Ms. Evans…Mr. Pratter, Jamie…everybody." She works the knot, untying the jacket. "I'm sorry for being careless."

"We're glad you're okay," says Ms. Evans.

"Clever problem-solving, Jamie," says Mr. Pratter. "You, too, Jeremy."

CHAPTER THIRTEEN

"I was so afraid Misha had hurt herself badly," says Beth as the girls eat lunch the next day.

"Same here," says Raina. "Then Jacket-rope Jamie came to the rescue." Jamie can't tell if it's a compliment or the opposite because Raina's voice sounds strange and her smile is crooked. It reminds Jamie of when she was Noah's partner in science.

Blushing and shaking her head, Jamie says, "Beth, we're going to the marina tonight to test *Seaker*. Wanna come?"

Before Beth answers, Jamie notices Jeremy standing behind them. When she glares at him, he hurries away.

"You make it sound like an adventure," says Beth, "but I've got ball tonight."

Mr. Pratter starts block 3 smiling directly at

Jamie. "Thanks to Jamie's project," he says, "and the National Film Board, we have Bill Mason's film *Paddle to the Sea* to watch this afternoon."

Yay!

Beth gives her a thumbs-up. Raina rolls her eyes. *What's with that?*

As Jamie watches Paddle on the screen, she pictures *Seaker* stuck in calm water and then swamped by rough waves. Jamie holds her breath as Paddle shoots over the edge of Niagara Falls and plummets through the mist. Paddle emerges—whole. Will *Seaker*?

When the film is over, Noah says, "We have the book at home. I think it's better than the movie."

"I think so too," says Raina.

"A movie can never include all the details a book can," says Mr. Pratter. "But the film certainly makes the dangers Paddle encounters more vivid."

Jamie wonders if *Seaker* will be able to survive the journey.

Like I need to worry more.

"And another thing's better in the movie," says Raina, looking at Noah. "Instead of just saying Paddle's maker is 'the Indian boy,' it calls him Kyle."

Jamie scrunches her face. "Yeah, that *is* weird

in the book. Lots of other people in the story have names."

Noah adds, "I like how both say he's a boy with a dream."

Jamie nods. *Having a dream is exciting.* Her smile fades when she realizes Raina is scowling at her.

Uncle Doug arrives at Jamie's after their early supper. The girls test *Seaker*'s equipment one more time, confirming it's tracking properly. They secure the antenna with duct tape and then use strip after strip of waterproof repair tape to seal the batteries and GPS inside the small boat. They also wrap tape around the transmitter and the base of the solar panel so water can't seep in.

Dad catches a ride down to the marina in Uncle Doug's truck with his fishing boat in tow. Mom, Brock and the girls follow in the family's truck.

At the marina, Mom says, "Brock's more interested in the zip line so we'll stay in the playground. But I'll take some photos when you're on the water."

The brothers launch the fishing boat, and then

they and the girls clamber in and put on life jackets. As Dad slowly motors out into the river, a boy rides a bike onto the dock. Jamie squints.

It's Jeremy. *He heard me invite Beth. He wants to see us fail so he can rub it in.*

Jamie clutches *Seaker*. Raina's holding the fishing pole, its line tied to the little boat. Jamie leans out and sets *Seaker* afloat. It bobs along, keeping stable. The ballast is doing its job.

Jamie and Uncle Doug hunch over his cell phone. She searches for the indicator showing *Seaker*'s location. "I can't see the dot, can you?"

"Nope." He taps the screen. "*Seaker*'s not tracking. Haul it in."

The girls groan. Raina reels in *Seaker* and Jamie plucks it from the river.

Slumping in her seat, Raina mutters, "Why isn't it working?"

Jamie pats Raina's shoulder. *If I can't get* Seaker *to work, Raina will be done with me.* Jamie fights to keep the panic out of her voice. "It's one more puzzle to solve. We can do this."

Raina nods. "Maybe something got disconnected when we did the wrapping."

Jamie's about to start peeling the waterproof

tape to look inside when Jeremy yells something from the dock.

"Do you know him, Jamie?" Dad asks.

"He's in our class."

Dad steers the boat toward the marina and shouts, "What did you say?"

Jeremy calls, "What's wrong with *Seaker*?"

"It stopped tracking," Uncle Doug yells.

"Check the transmitter. Sometimes the switch on that brand doesn't stay on."

Sure enough, it's off. Jamie flips the switch. "Check your phone again, Uncle Doug."

"It's tracking," he says.

Jamie shouts, "Thanks."

Raina arches her eyebrows. "Who knew Jeremy could be helpful?"

After drying *Seaker* extremely carefully, Jamie securely duct-tapes the transmitter switch so it will stay on. She adds layers of repair tape. Raina returns *Seaker* to the water, where it cruises along behind them, sending a clear signal to Uncle Doug's cell phone.

To test how waterproof *Seaker* is, they head out into rougher water for a while. The little boat flips around, then rights itself. Each time a wave hides it from view, Jamie gasps. But when they eventually return to the dock and haul in *Seaker*, she's relieved it's still tracking. Once they towel it off and hold it upside down, there's no sign of any moisture inside.

The next morning, Mr. Pratter asks Jamie and Raina to update the class about their project.

Jamie's knees quiver only a little as she walks to the front of the class. Beth's smile boosts her courage. "Beth helped us come up with the name *Seaker*—S-e-*a*-k-e-r—for our boat. The equipment all works and we're launching *Seaker* on Saturday—"

"We're almost done making a website to track where it goes," says Raina. "We'll add photos too."

"Send me the link, Jamie," says the teacher. "I'll post it on our class website so we can all follow *Seaker*'s progress."

Back at her desk, Jamie types the URL for Mr. Pratter on her assigned laptop. *How many kids will care? Will Jeremy?*

When Jamie arrives at the school's year-end family barbecue, Raina and Beth are already there, deep in conversation.

"...wish she'd stop smiling at him all—" Raina turns. "Oh, hi, Jamie."

Is she talking about me smiling at Noah? Jamie's about to ask when Raina jumps up to introduce her parents to Jamie's. Beth introduces her mom, and the other two girls in grade 4 arrive.

The adults arrange their lawn chairs together. Brock and his friend Ruby are playing tag with the other JK kids.

All of the girls park themselves on one blanket to eat.

Noah saunters by with his plate loaded.

Misha asks, "Jamie, will *Seaker* go under the Nipigon River Bridge?"

Noah stops behind her, crunching a carrot stick and listening.

Misha's so friendly. I should invite her over sometime. Jamie doesn't smile at her in case Raina thinks it's aimed at Noah. "Yes, if all goes as planned." She explains *Seaker*'s route.

"We gotta all be on the bridge to see that," says Noah.

"Yup, you should," says Raina.

"I'll definitely come," says Beth.

Misha adds, "Jamie, let us know when, okay?"

A man towers over Jamie. "So you're the *Seaker* girl, eh? I've heard lots about your project from my son. Good luck."

"Thanks."

As he walks away, Jamie whispers, "Who was that?"

"Mr. Kane," says Raina. "Jeremy's dad."

Jeremy told his father about Seaker*?*

Two more adults appear. "Hi, Jamie. All the best with your project," says the woman. "I'm Ruby's mom. Brock's *so* excited about what you're doing with his boat."

"Wow, Jamie," says Beth. "You're famous."

Raina's staring at something in the grass. Then she looks up, halfway smiling. "At least Noah might show up at the bridge. Even if he doesn't know how much I'm part of the project."

CHAPTER FOURTEEN

On the last day of school, Jamie's class eats lunch outside. Then Jamie heads to the playground with Raina and Beth.

"I wish I could come along to launch *Seaker* tomorrow," says Beth as she and Raina climb to the top of the monkey bars. "But we're driving to Thunder Bay to stay until Sunday. Boring Grandma time."

"Beth—she's your elder," exclaims Raina. "You need to be respectful."

"I know, but all she does is complain about her bunions and arthritis, and that we haven't moved to Thunder Bay to look after—"

"You're moving?" Raina and Jamie ask in unison.

"No. At least I don't think so," she grumbles. "I hope not."

"Me too," says Raina.

Jamie adds, "Same here."

Before block 3 starts, Jamie checks her email and almost squeals. The LU professor replied: "Thank you for bringing this to my attention. Robogals sounds like an interesting and educational program. Once the fall term is under way, we'll explore student interest, but there is no guarantee."

One step closer.

Launch day is finally here. Uncle Doug, Raina and Jamie's family drive to the creek Jamie picked out. It's sunny, but the western sky is darkening. With *Seaker* nestled in Dad's backpack, they hike to the creek. When Brock leaps over a tree root, a squirrel scurries up to a high branch and barks at him.

At the creek, Jamie and Raina hold *Seaker* above their heads while Mom takes a photograph.

Jamie calls, "Uncle Doug and Brock, come stand with us." Mom snaps several shots.

Uncle Doug confirms the GPS is tracking.

"Here goes." Jamie steps onto a flat rock in the creek, crouches and launches the boat. The current snatches *Seaker* away. They watch until the bright red boat disappears around the bend.

"We did it!" Jamie hugs Raina. "*Seaker*'s on its way."

While hiking back to the road, the girls track the boat using Dad's cell phone. It travels quickly down the creek on its way to the Nipigon River.

"I wish we had data on our phones so we could follow *Seaker* all the time," says Raina.

As they drive toward town, clouds billow. Raindrops splat.

Branches wave in the wind.

Jamie shudders. *Will* Seaker *keep going?*

At Jamie's house, the girls take over the computer so they can post the launch photos on their website.

"Look," says Raina, "*Seaker* already has fourteen followers."

"Who?" asks Jamie. Besides themselves, the list has their parents, Uncle Doug, Mr. Pratter, Beth, Misha, Noah and three usernames they don't recognize.

The girls track *Seaker*'s progress.

Jamie groans. "Why's it moving so slow?"

"It all depends on the current, wind and waves," says Dad, peering at the screen. "Supper's ready."

Mom sets out plates and napkins. Dad serves the simple meal he made of sandwiches and raw veggies and dip.

Raina raises a hand to her mouth to hide her grimace from the adults.

Oh no—egg salad.

Raina dips her head toward Jamie and mumbles, "Is this payback for lunches?" She eyes her plate. "At least they're fresh."

Jamie blushes.

After they finish supper, Jamie says, "Let's check how far *Seaker* is now." She and Raina dart back to the computer.

Raina shrieks, pointing at the first comment. "Beth wrote: 'Good luck, Seaker!'"

"Cool." Jamie smiles.

When Raina goes home, she promises to come back first thing in the morning.

CHAPTER FIFTEEN

The jangling of Jamie's cell phone wakes her on Sunday morning. Daylight peeks around the edges of her blinds.

She doesn't recognize the number. Throwing off the covers, she sits on the edge of the bed. "Hello?"

"Something's wrong with *Seaker*," says a boy's voice.

"What? Who is this?"

"Jeremy."

How'd he get my phone number? "Uh—"

"Jamie, check the website."

"Okay, bye."

She dashes to the computer, where Mom is reading email. "There's a problem with *Seaker*. Can you go to our website, please?"

They study the map. Mom says, "*Seaker*'s at the

edge of the river. I don't see a problem."

"But it's been sending the same GPS signal for hours. It must be stuck." Jamie starts tapping her phone. "I'll call Raina and Uncle Doug. We have to get it back in the current."

After a quick breakfast, Jamie's family picks up Raina. Following Uncle Doug, they drive to a spot close to where the boat appears to be.

Uncle Doug checks his phone. "Signal's fading. It's likely stuck in the shade. We need to hurry."

They battle through the underbrush. Branches whip Jamie's face and thistles scratch her arms. Tears well up. *We can't lose* Seaker *before it even reaches Lake Superior.*

After twenty minutes of slogging, they reach the riverbank. Uncle Doug glances up and down the river. "We've got to be close. But the signal stopped. Search carefully."

They fan out, checking under bushes overhanging the river.

"Don't lean over so far, Brock," Jamie yells. "You might—"

He stumbles, tries to grab a branch but misses. *Splash!*

"I'm coming, Brock," Jamie yells as she runs

toward him. He's coughing and struggling to stand. He barely learned how to swim last summer. Thankfully the water here is circling in a slow eddy, not a strong current.

Jamie leaps into the river and grabs Brock. The water's up past her knees. She tries to haul him up, but she loses her grip and he falls backward.

Raina jumps in. The girls each take hold of one of Brock's arms. They lift him to his feet, pushing him toward the adults on the riverbank. Dad reaches for Brock while the girls heave him upward. Mom and Uncle Doug help the girls scramble out.

Brock shivers uncontrollably. "Th-th-thanks, J-J-Jamie…R-R-Raina."

Dad and Mom argue about who was supposed to be watching Brock while Mom strips off Brock's sopping clothes. She wraps her jacket around him.

"Thank you, girls." Mom brushes away tears. "Good teamwork."

Dad hugs Jamie. "You both were so brave."

Uncle Doug wrings out Brock's clothes.

"We have to get you three home and into dry clothes." Mom motions to Jamie. "Come on. We're leaving."

"We can't go!" Jamie says. "What about *Seaker*?"

Mom frowns. "What's more important?"

"I-I'm o-k-k-ay, Mom," Brock says. "I s-saw something red like *Seaker*. In those t-tangled-up branches." He points to a spot near where he fell. "We gotta ch-check there."

Jamie and Raina hustle over to the edge.

"Get back here," hollers Mom.

But Jamie lies on her stomach and slips her arm between twigs and tree roots. "Found it! Good eye, Brock." Jamie passes the boat to Raina before standing up.

Raina cradles *Seaker*. "The top layer of tape's ripped in one spot, but that's easy to fix once it's dry."

"Let's move into that sunny patch to recharge the batteries and warm the kids up," Uncle Doug says.

Everyone finds a log or rock to sit on. Jamie removes her shoes. Then she peels off her socks, squeezes out the water and drapes them over a branch. Raina follows her lead.

Jamie's relieved and happy that Brock is safe— and her phone stayed dry—but she feels sick that the boat got stuck so close to home.

Mom passes around trail mix. "What a glum bunch."

Jamie bites off a hangnail. "What if we can't get *Seaker* working again?"

"We will," Raina says.

But if we can't, maybe you won't be my friend anymore.

"You know what?" Raina balances a jack-pine cone on her fingertip. "It doesn't matter if it *never* works again. *Seaker* is the most epic fun I've ever had."

Jamie's words are missing again. She grins, feeling silly for doubting Raina's friendship.

Dad's napping with his hat covering his face.

Brock asks the girls, "Wanna play I Spy?"

"Okay," says Jamie.

He giggles. "I spy somethin' that is green."

"Ha, ha," says Raina. "There's a million green things." She offers to play a clapping game with him.

After the trail mix bag is empty and Dad wakes up, Uncle Doug announces, "Batteries are fully charged."

The equipment is all functioning again. Jamie pulls the repair tape out of Dad's backpack and re-tapes the keel, adding an extra layer.

Everyone moves to the riverbank.

"Your turn to launch it, Raina," Jamie says.

When Raina lets go of the boat, Jamie calls, "Bon voyage, *Seaker*."

At Jamie's house, the girls keep checking the website. *Seaker* carries on to the end of the first part of the Nipigon River.

"Dad," Jamie says, "*Seaker*'s in Lake Helen now. When do you think it'll reach the highway bridge? We want to watch it pass underneath."

He glances out the window. "It's hard to say with the rain coming, but I'm guessing around three o'clock."

Jamie pulls out her phone. "Raina, when does Beth get home?"

"By lunchtime."

"I'll call her now. Can you call Misha and Noah?"

"Sure." She grins.

Right away Beth asks about *Seaker* and Jamie fills her in. "I'm happy you can come to the bridge… that you *want* to come."

"I have to admit, *Seaker* is really impressive."

"Wow—thanks. We'll pick you up."

Raina and Jamie add an invitation to the website so people can join them.

Will anyone else come in the rain? Will Seaker *even make it?*

CHAPTER SIXTEEN

The rain eases as they drive toward the four-lane bridge. To the right stands the single-track Canadian Pacific Railway bridge.

Jamie, squished between Beth and Raina, nudges them both. "Look at all the people!" The girls whoop.

Cars and trucks line both sides of the highway by the bridge. People are streaming to the north side, spreading out along the walkway.

After Mom parks, the girls head toward the bridge. Jamie's insides feel like they're sinking and flying at the same time. She grasps both girls' hands, giving them a squeeze. "I'm all nervous-cited," she says, which gets them giggling.

Raina points out the town librarian near Mr. Pratter on the walkway. Most of their class is here.

Even Jeremy. When he notices the girls, he calls and waves them over.

The sight of a police car driving up to the bridge startles Jamie.

It stops and two officers march over to the walkway. "Good afternoon, folks," one says loudly. "What's going on?"

"You'll need to talk to my student, Jamie Sola," says Mr. Pratter, pointing her way.

Jamie lifts her hand, heart pounding. The officers step closer. Her tongue feels paralyzed.

"It's a science experiment," Dad says.

"Go on."

"You see—"

"It's okay, Dad." Jamie sucks in a breath. Knees trembling, she explains. Then, blushing, she adds, "I didn't expect so many people to show up."

One of the officers returns to the police car and pulls out the public address microphone. "Everyone can stay on the bridge," he says. His voice is amplified so the crowd hears every word. "As long as you don't block traffic."

The officers stay to keep order…and to watch.

People jam together along the outer railing, straining to glimpse bright red in the river. Mom keeps a grip on Brock's hand. Cars, semi-trailers and logging trucks whoosh past, rumbling over the long bridge.

"*Seaker* should appear any minute," Uncle Doug says, checking his phone.

Finally Brock points and shouts, "There's *Seaker*!"

The tiny boat skims into view. Jamie's heart swells at the sight. It's in the strong current in the middle of the river but staying upright. The crowd cheers as *Seaker* approaches.

A woman aims a long-lens camera, and dozens of phones capture photos.

All too soon *Seaker* glides out of sight below the highway bridge. People clap and whistle, urging it onward.

Jamie wants to relive the moment. She wishes she could be on the other side of the bridge to see when *Seaker* gets there. *If only I had X-ray vision—*

In a flash, Jeremy climbs over the two railings between the walkway and the highway.

He must wish the same thing. Sure enough, he checks for traffic, then starts crossing the westbound lanes.

"Jeremy, come back!" She tugs Mr. Pratter's sleeve. "You gotta stop him."

Mr. Pratter and the nearby police officer leap the railings and dash after Jeremy.

On the public address microphone, the other officer commands, "Everyone stay on the walkway."

Jeremy is about to climb the railing to reach the eastbound lanes when Mr. Pratter and the officer grasp his arms. They guide him back over the railings to safety next to Jamie.

"Stay off the highway, young man," the officer orders.

"Sorry," Jeremy says. "I...I wanted to see *Seaker* again."

After the adults move away, Jamie tells Jeremy, "I know—I wanted to go too."

The officer at the police car says through the mic, "Keep on the walkway to leave the bridge."

Uncle Doug studies his phone. "*Seaker* just passed under the railway bridge."

Jamie beams.

"Good job," Jeremy says.

"Thanks." Jamie tips her head sideways. "I'm surprised you even came. Didn't you think I'd fail?"

"I only said that 'cause..." He inches closer to Jamie. "'Cause I wish *I'd* been the one to think of making *Seaker*." He takes off before she can reply.

Noah fist-bumps Jamie, saying, "It *can* be done—you're awesome!" But he doesn't say anything to Raina.

Weird.

"Thanks, and Raina's awesome too," says Jamie and turns to her. "We did it!" Jamie high-fives Raina, Beth, Misha and all the rest of their classmates.

The woman with the camera introduces herself. She's a reporter for the *Nipigon-Red Rock Gazette*. She asks to take their photo. "Jamie and Raina, could you stand in the middle, with your friends around you?" She organizes the group so they can all get in the picture and steps back. "All right, one, two, three, CHEER."

Everyone screams, arms raised.

"Another one," says the reporter. "This time, say, '*Seaker*.'" She snaps more. "Thank you. Look for yourselves in the *Gazette* and the Thunder Bay newspaper." She moves near Jamie and Raina. "Your parents gave me permission to ask you some questions for an article. Are you willing to do an interview?"

"Definitely," Raina says.

Is there anything *Raina's afraid of?* Jamie adds, "Okay."

The reporter asks Jamie how she came up with the idea and if she'd done anything like this before. She quizzes Raina about how she got involved in the project. Then she asks, "What was the most challenging part?"

All Jamie can think of is when Raina backed out. But she doesn't want to say that. What else? Deciding to use Brock's boat? Finding the equipment? Getting the tracking to work?

Raina laughs. "Fishing Jamie's little brother out of the Nipigon River."

Whew—thanks for coming up with something.

Of course, the reporter wants to hear the whole story as she scribbles notes.

Jamie says, "Actually *Seaker* getting stuck there *was* the hardest part, not knowing if we'd find it. And when we did, not knowing if the tracking would work again. I was afraid *Seaker* would never make it even this far."

After they answer the reporter's questions, she says, "I'll try to squeeze this into Tuesday's *Gazette*, but it might take another week."

"Thanks a lot," says Raina.

It's 6:48 a.m. on Monday and Jamie's wide awake imagining where *Seaker* is now. She slips out of bed and creeps down the hallway to turn on the computer. It takes forever to start up. Finally she goes to *Seaker*'s website, clicks the map and gasps. The little boat's in the wide part of the Nipigon River, halfway to Red Rock. "Yes!" she exclaims, then whispers, "Sorry" toward her sleeping family's bedrooms.

Raina's idea was whoever gets up first should text the other. As Jamie types into her phone, it beeps with Raina's incoming message. They text back and forth several times.

Mom appears. "You're up early. How's *Seaker*?"

"Still moving and tracking."

"Wonderful. Want some toast?"

"Sure."

Soon Dad and Brock join them to eat breakfast together, and then Dad goes to work.

Mom's phone rings in her bedroom. It takes her four rings to answer. Muffled voice. Returning, she says, "Believe it or not, that was a Thunder Bay radio station. They want to interview you about *Seaker* and…"

Jamie's insides feel as cold as a lunar night. *Me talk on the radio?*

Mom's still speaking. "…I have to get back to them with a time."

"What about Raina? She should be part of it too."

"Can you call her?"

Raina's response to the interview request is no surprise. "Duh, of course we'll do it. You and me are rock stars!"

Jamie *has* to do the interview. She can't let Raina down. Mom arranges for the interviewer to call her cell tomorrow at 10:30 a.m. Jamie's insides thaw to fridge temperature when she hears it will be recorded. If—no, *when*—she messes up, they can take out those parts. They'll probably need all day to get it ready for Wednesday's morning show.

CHAPTER SEVENTEEN

By Tuesday—interview day—*Seaker* passes Red Rock and heads south into more open water.

Raina shows up at ten. The girls are hyper-nervous and pace around the living room. They're talking over each other and getting louder by the second. Mom says, "Okay, you two, outside. Run around the block. Go."

Raina has a head start as she forgot to take off her shoes when she arrived. But Jamie catches up to her after the first corner. By the time they get back to the house, they're less hyper. After Mom sets Brock up watching a video in her bedroom, she joins the girls at the kitchen table.

When the phone rings, Mom answers and puts it on speaker.

This is it. Jamie's whole body quivers.

The interviewer introduces herself and gets them all laughing immediately. She starts the recording and asks the regular questions: how Jamie got the idea for the project, what equipment they're using, the launch details and where *Seaker* is now. Then she asks, "Jamie, why was making *Seaker* important?"

"Uh…um…" *Uh-oh. Does she mean important to me or important because we're proving it can be done?*

Raina nudges Jamie in the ribs, mouthing words she can't decipher.

Jamie stares at the phone, gripping the edge of the table. "It was…uh…more than just fun. It was showing that making a trackable boat could be done. At first I freaked out when I couldn't find a model design. Then I got the idea to use a toy boat. And it turned out okay, uh, kind of special. And lots of people are following *Seaker* now. That makes it way better."

"Thank you, Jamie. How about you, Raina?"

"It was important because Jamie dreamed big—small boat, big adventure. And I got to be part of it, and it makes me want to do more projects with Jamie. We can't wait to see how far *Seaker* goes.

And if it wasn't for Jamie and *Seaker*, I wouldn't be thinking I could be an engineer someday. And…I guess that's it."

"Thank you both so much. I really appreciate your sharing your experience." The woman wraps up the interview giving their names and the *Seaker* website. "Okay, the recording's done. That was excellent. This will air tomorrow morning about 8:20. Thanks again."

They all say goodbye and Mom ends the call. "Congratulations, girls. That was great."

Jamie groans. "Except for my speechless part."

"I guess it's a good thing it wasn't live," says Mom.

"Hey, Raina," says Jamie. "I didn't know you want to be an engineer."

Raina turns from staring out the window and says quietly, "I didn't either until I thought about her question."

After Raina leaves, Jamie calls Uncle Doug and tells him when the interview will be on the radio.

"I'll be listening," he says. "Great article in today's *Gazette*."

"Right—it's Tuesday. I totally forgot about the *Gazette*. We haven't got ours yet."

"That's my niece, junior scientist and celebrity. Thanks for mentioning me, but you didn't need to."

"We couldn't have done it without you."

"Maybe, maybe not."

Jamie giggles. "Thanks."

The next morning, Raina, Beth and Jamie gather at Jamie's at eight. They sit around the table eating muffins and cheese and grapes and listening to the radio.

At 8:20, some guy is still talking about the stock market. Finally a familiar voice begins speaking.

Jamie squeals. "That's our interviewer."

The woman introduces the story about *Seaker*, then says, "I'm delighted to play this interview recorded yesterday with the two grade four students in Nipigon. We talked about their trackable boat." Mom turns up the radio as Jamie and Raina answer the first question.

Do I really sound like that?

Beth is riveted. Everyone is, even Brock. They removed Jamie's long pause so well, it was as if it never happened. *Whew.*

But something's not right. A few of Raina's answers are missing. And her last one is cut off. All they left in was: "It was important because Jamie dreamed big—small boat, big adventure."

Jamie peeks at Raina. Her eyes are shiny. She looks crushed.

As soon as the interview is over, cheers erupt from everyone else. Dad grabs his truck keys. "Good job, girls—that was worth being late for work." He heads out the door.

Beth, sitting between Jamie and Raina, pulls them both into a group hug. "Jamie, you sure talked a *lot*."

Raina grimaces.

"I—" Before Jamie can answer, her phone rings. It's Uncle Doug, practically shouting. "Congratulations, you two—well done."

Jamie thanks him but can't tell Raina what he said because she's gone.

CHAPTER EIGHTEEN

Jamie dashes outside. Raina and Beth are in the driveway, strapping on their bike helmets.

Beth says, "Raina, tell me what's wrong."

"I just wanna get out of here."

"Raina, wait!" Jamie runs up to them. "No fair your answers got left out."

Turning away, Raina swipes at a tear.

Beth puts her hand on Raina's back. "How much was left out?"

"Almost half," says Raina.

"Why?" Beth asks.

Jamie moves in front of Raina, looking into her red, puffy eyes. "The stuff you said was *great*. It should've been on the radio."

"Yup, it *should've* been," says Raina, her voice catching. "But it's not just—"

"Jamie!" calls a boy speeding down the hill on his bike. He skids into the driveway, spraying gravel. It's Noah. "Jamie, you did really good in the interview. Your project's *so* amazing," he says.

Jamie glances at Raina. "Thanks, Noah, but—"

Raina takes off, pedalling hard. Beth zooms after her.

"What's with them?" asks Noah.

"Raina's upset they left out part of her interview."

"Yeah, I noticed it was mostly you."

"She helped a *lot* with *Seaker*." *I need to text her.*

"I gotta go." Jamie turns and leaps up the steps.

Inside, Jamie snatches her phone. **I know you're upset about Noah. I can't believe they cut half your answers.**😠

She waits, expecting Raina to text back as soon as she gets home. But after several minutes, there's no reply. *She should be home by now.*

Fingers trembling, Jamie sends another text.

Five minutes pass.

Raina doesn't respond.

Maybe they went to Beth's.

Jamie waits until she's sure they've had enough time to reach Beth's house. She calls Raina's number, but there's no answer. Now Jamie's annoyed and breathing fast, wishing they'd never done the interview. *No fair blaming me. The radio station edited it.*

Jamie punches out a text to Beth: **Did Raina get my text?**

Beth replies: **Yes.**

She didn't text back.

Right.

Why is she ignoring me?

Beth answers: **Mad about what you did.**

I didn't shorten her answers.

It was YOUR answers.

Jamie blows hard. **What was wrong with them?**

You never said we. It was all me and I—like Raina didn't count.

Jamie replays the interview in her head.

She moans like she's been slugged in the stomach.

It's true. Jamie was so nervous doing the interview she didn't think about how she worded her answers.

Not one mention of working with Raina. Shame burns to her core.

I'm the absolute worst friend in the world. Tears spring to her eyes.

She texts Raina: **I'm really really sorry I didn't include you** 😢

She waits several minutes. No reply.

She calls Beth.

No answer.

Jamie calls Raina's number.

She doesn't answer.

I have to find them. Jamie slaps on her helmet, jumps on her bike and rides to Raina's house.

No bikes outside. *Must be at Beth's.*

Jamie races the two blocks to Beth's house. Both girls' bikes are lying on the grass. Jamie drops hers beside them.

She presses the doorbell and gulps a deep breath.

Beth answers the door. "Raina doesn't want to see you."

"I need to talk to her."

Beth starts closing the door. "She's not your friend anymore."

CHAPTER NINETEEN

Raina isn't my friend anymore? Jamie's dizzy, like the oxygen is all sucked out of her. She crumples on the step.

Every time something went wrong with *Seaker*, Jamie feared this. But when they were waiting by the river for the batteries to recharge, Raina said she'd had the most epic fun ever. Jamie thought she *finally* had a real friend.

Now she's done with me. Beth probably isn't my friend anymore, either.

Her chest and throat squeeze tight.

Beep. A text. Did Raina change her mind?

It's Mom. She's going grocery shopping with Brock.

When Jamie stands up, she still feels woozy, so she pushes her bike instead of riding it.

At home, she bellyflops on her bed. The house is empty, and Jamie sobs over losing her friends.

After she cries herself out, Jamie rolls onto her back and takes some deep breaths.

I have to apologize to Raina. But she won't talk to me, so how can I?

Jamie could text again. Or leave a voice message. *No, that's lame.*

Then she remembers what Mom said when Jamie was eight and accidentally broke their neighbour's fancy vase. "When you need to apologize, put it in writing." Jamie needs to write Raina a letter. An old-fashioned sorry on paper. Jamie must do the best, most sincere writing of her life so Raina knows she means it.

At her desk, she writes:

Dear Raina,

*I am SO SO sorry. I didn't mean to leave you out of my answers. I was mega-nervous and my brain didn't think clearly. You ~~were~~ are super important in **our** Seaker project. I get why you're upset. If you answered like me, my feelings would be hurt bad. I am REALLY sorry.*

I still want to be your friend,

Jamie

She folds the paper and tucks it inside an envelope. Feeling a ripple of hope, she pedals to Raina's, sees no bikes and returns to Beth's house.

Beth's mom comes to the door. "Hi, Jamie, I heard you on the radio—"

"Is Raina here?" Jamie clutches the letter. "It's important."

"I'll get her."

"Thanks. Please don't tell her it's me."

Beth's mom gives her a quizzical look. "Uh, okay."

When both girls appear, Jamie hands Raina the letter. "Please read this."

"Don't you get it, Jamie?" says Beth. "Raina doesn't want anything to do with you."

Jamie, eyes brimming with tears, ignores Beth and pleads with Raina to open the envelope.

Raina huffs. "You had *no* problem telling our class that Beth helped name *Seaker*." She glares at Jamie. "But you didn't say *anything* in the interview about all my help."

"I know, I—"

"Not. One. Thing."

"I feel awful. I was nervous." Jamie's crying and her voice turns squeaky. "I made a mistake, okay? Please, read my letter."

Instead, Raina throws the envelope on the floor. "You want *all* the attention, don't you? From Mr. Pratter, the interviewer, parents, Noah—"

"That's *so* not true!" says Jamie, raising her voice.

Raina opens her mouth to speak, but Jamie's faster. "You've *never* had to be the new girl. And *nothing* makes you nervous. You can talk to *anyone*. All I want is a friend, but you two sure don't make it easy."

Jamie gulps a breath and blinks hard. "I gave up going to the district meet for you, Beth, but you're still always trying to hog Raina. And Raina, you keep wanting me to eat your gross egg sandwiches when you know I hate them!"

Raina and Beth both gape at her, eyes round as satellite dishes.

Shoot, I've said too much.

Or not enough. "I know I'm not perfect. But neither are you."

Jamie whirls, heart thumping, and rides away.

When it's time for supper, Jamie tells Mom, "I'm not hungry. I have a headache."

"Must be the heat. Go lie down and I'll bring you a cool cloth."

Jamie stretches out on her bed.

"Jamie?" It's Brock. "I can do the dishwasher for you."

"Thanks, buddy."

After supper, Jamie hears Mom return to her art studio while Dad and Brock leave for a bike ride.

Jamie curls up on her side. *Will Raina read my letter? If she does, will she believe it?*

It takes forever for her to fall asleep. Three times she sits up in the dark, quaking. She pictures Raina's shocked face and feels ashamed. *I wish I didn't say all those things. I'll never make a friend in this town.*

All morning she's focused on her phone, waiting to hear from Raina. No text. No call.

Jamie and her family drive to Red Rock for the Canada Day celebrations. They arrive in time to see the end of the parade and sing "O Canada" as the flag is raised.

Jamie scans the crowd, wondering if Raina and Beth came too. A woman Mom's age is pointing at Jamie during the anthem, making her squirm.

Afterward, the woman weaves through the crowd to Jamie, saying, "Hello—you're the Paddle-to-the-Sea girl, right?"

"I'm one of the *Seaker* girls. Yes, *Seaker* is following Paddle's water trail."

"Right, *Seaker*. I saw you in the *Gazette* and heard your interview. Congratulations—I'm so impressed."

"Thanks, I—"

About ten steps away, Raina and Beth are walking arm in arm, laughing. When they see Jamie, they veer left, disappearing into the crowd.

Jamie's stomach clenches. *If Raina read my letter, it didn't make any difference.*

The woman is chatting away. "I even have the site bookmarked on my phone so I can follow *Seaker*'s journey."

She checks out the website right then and there. "Okay, so I'm looking at the map now. Shouldn't the currents be taking *Seaker* south or southwest, away from us? It's near Lamb Island but moving north."

"What?" Jamie stares at the small screen. Sure enough, *Seaker* is backtracking. Jamie panics. As if she doesn't have enough to worry about.

CHAPTER TWENTY

When Jamie tells her family about *Seaker*, they're disappointed. "I'm sad," says Brock, hugging her. She worries about the little boat and Raina the rest of the day and part of the night. Then she wakes up with a stomach ache.

And an idea for how she can fix the interview disaster.

Jamie finds the radio station phone number. Before she chickens out, she calls and asks for the interviewer. As the woman says hello, Jamie blurts, "This is Jamie Sola, from Nipigon."

"Hi, Jamie, nice to hear from you. What's up?"

"I *really* need your help. Raina's answers on the radio were shortened a whole lot. And she's super upset. Could you please add her full answers to the recording on your website? *Please*?"

The interviewer kindly says, "I'll see what I can do. Check the website tomorrow."

"Thank you so much."

"How's *Seaker* doing?"

"Uh…not great. It seems stuck or backtracking."

"Sorry to hear that. Call me if it gets close to Thunder Bay, okay?"

"Sure." They say goodbye.

Jamie keeps tracking *Seaker*. She's desperate to know why the boat's travelling northeast. Did it get caught in a fishing net? Is a moose carrying it in its antlers? A few times when she checks, *Seaker* drifts southward for a while. Maybe it's stuck in a giant whirlpool.

She wants to talk with Raina about it. Does Raina even know there's a problem with *Seaker*? Does she care?

Their friendship is *totally* off course too. Tears roll down Jamie's cheeks. *If only time travel was real— I'd go back three days and rescue our friendship.*

She blows her nose. *How can I rescue* Seaker*? Should I ask Uncle Doug to take me out in his boat?* After composing a text to him, she cancels it, remembering he planned to go fishing today.

She's queasy. Is this the end of *Seaker*'s journey?

There's nothing you can do about this, she sternly tells herself.

She takes some shuddery breaths and decides to wait an hour before checking again. Jamie sets an alarm on her phone and hops on her bike. Maybe pedalling fast around town will help.

After a few blocks, another idea for how she can make things right with Raina pops into her head. Jamie squeezes her brakes, straddles her bike and pulls out her phone. She sends a text, praying it will work.

Late afternoon, Jamie sprawls on the couch, staring out the window. *How could so many things go wrong so fast?*

"Jamie?" says Brock, patting her leg. "Scoot wants to cheer you up about *Seaker*." He gently hands over his cheetah stuffie.

"Thanks, buddy." As Jamie cuddles Scoot, a tear drips on his fur. She wipes it dry with her hand.

CHAPTER TWENTY-ONE

The next morning, when Jamie checks *Seaker*'s position (still messed up), there's a comment from Jeremy. "I figured Engineer Raina must have had more to say!" He included a link. Jamie clicks it and the full-length radio interview is now up. *Will Raina see it?*

An hour later, Jamie's phone beeps. It's a text from Beth: **Raina's still mad at you. 😠 But she's upset about Seaker. She wants to know what's wrong.**

Jamie replies: **I'm worried too. I meant every word in my letter. 🥺**

Raina still cares about Seaker. *Maybe there's hope for me.*

Jamie pedals to Raina's and rings the doorbell. Mr. Larouche opens the door.

"Hi, Jamie. I'll get Raina for you."

But Beth shows up, in pyjamas. Sadness pinches Jamie's throat. *A sleepover. Without me.*

"Why are you here?" Beth's voice is flat. "My text wasn't an invitation."

"I need to talk to Raina."

"She hasn't changed her mind."

"Beth, you gotta help me. I need to apologize to her."

"Yes, you really do." She sighs. "What you said about me hogging Raina was mean—"

"Sorry, I—"

Beth holds her hand up to silence Jamie. "But you're right. And I know what it's like to be the new girl. That was me in JK. Raina pulled me over to the dress-up corner. She put silly outfits on us and we laughed."

"Yeah, she's kind like that. She must have made you feel so good. It's *awful* being the new kid." Jamie reaches out and touches Beth's arm. "Can you please get her for me?"

"I'll try."

The wait feels like hours.

Then Beth's back with Raina, who stands in front of Jamie, arms folded.

Jamie breathes deeply. "Raina, I'm extremely sorry. Did you read my letter?"

"Just now. After you texted Beth about it."

As Beth gives Raina a sideways hug, Raina uncrosses her arms. "And Noah texted me. Said some nice things about me helping with *Seaker*. Did you ask him to do that?"

"Yeah. It bugged me he never said anything to you."

Raina's lips are squished together, her eyebrows scrunched.

"You have to believe me," says Jamie. "I never meant to not talk about you in the interview. You're a huge part of making *Seaker*."

"It was bad enough they left out most of what I said," says Raina in a low tone. "But you leaving me out hurt my feelings a *lot*."

Jamie's crying now. "I'm really sorry I hurt you."

Raina sniffles and shifts closer to Jamie. "Thanks."

"I should have talked about all *we* did," says Jamie. "All *you* did."

"Yup." After an awkward silence, Raina adds, "I know you didn't do it on purpose."

"You're right."

"But you can't change what you said."

"I know, Raina. But at least the whole interview is uploaded now, like I asked."

"You got them to do that?"

"Yeah, I—"

"Jamie, you're a good friend."

"You are too."

Raina pulls her into a hug.

Jamie exhales relief and joy.

Looking at the ceiling, Beth thumps her hand on her heart and sighs. "The sweet reunion of the nerd squad."

Raina laughs and steps back. "Now if we could only figure out what's up with *Seaker*."

Jamie shares her theories.

"Maybe it got stuck and someone picked it up," adds Raina.

Beth says, "What if an eagle was fishing and snatched *Seaker* instead?"

"No!" exclaim both Jamie and Raina.

After Jamie goes home, it's a long day—with texts flying between all three girls, anxiously waiting to see what happens to the little boat.

CHAPTER TWENTY-TWO

All through Sunday there's no improvement with *Seaker*. But when Jamie checks the website on Monday morning, she shouts, "Woo-hoo!" The boat is almost at the Sleeping Giant rock formation near Thunder Bay.

Mom and Brock come running. Jamie exclaims, "*Seaker*'s heading southwest again!" She clasps Brock's hands and they jump in a celebration dance. Mom draws them into a group hug.

Jamie rechecks *Seaker*'s location—just to be sure—then calls Raina. Next Dad, followed by Uncle Doug and Beth. Then she remembers to call the radio interviewer. The woman is amazed to hear *Seaker*'s location.

"Jamie, can I call you in half an hour for a short interview? With Raina?"

Here's my chance to totally fix my mistake. "I'll check with her and call you right back."

Raina sounds wary but agrees, so Jamie confirms the interview time. Raina comes over ten minutes ahead.

During the interview, Jamie talks about Raina being a key part of the project and lets Raina answer questions first and say as much as she wants. By the end, all three are laughing. The interviewer promises the entire recording will be aired—nothing left out—and says goodbye.

"That was fun," says Raina on her way out the door. "Thanks, Jamie."

Whew—success!

After lunch, Jamie bikes to Raina's house and finds her and Beth busy on the computer.

Raina says, "I'm going to science camp in Thunder Bay in August." She checks the camp website. "There are only two spots left. You've got to come with me."

Jamie laughs.

"Hey, I'm serious. Why are you laughing?"

"'Cause my mom wanted to register me the day we found out my Dad got the job here. I said no."

Raina looks horrified. "Why would you *do* that?"

"I'd convinced myself I didn't like science anymore."

Raina snorts. "Like *that* could ever be true. Call your mom right now to get you in."

Jamie phones and asks. Her jaw drops. "What do you mean?" Pause. "Okay, thanks, Mom." Jamie ends the call and squeals.

"What just happened?" Beth asks.

"I can't register…because I'm already in. Mom signed me up in May hoping I'd change my mind."

"Excellent," says Raina.

Beth clears her throat. "Watching you two making *Seaker* has been so much fun, I'd like to give science camp a try."

"Really?" Raina's eyes bulge.

Jamie says, "Yeah! You *have* to come."

"Great." Beth grins. "I should've said this before, Jamie, but I'm truly glad you moved to Nipigon."

"Same here," says Jamie. *Never* ever *thought I'd feel this way.*

She accesses the Robogals website. "Take a look."

Raina and Beth study the page.

"Whoa," says Raina, "this looks awesome. When's the next workshop?"

"More like, when's the first one," says Jamie. "I emailed the LU professor in charge of engineering—"

Beth gasps. "You, Jamie Sola, emailed a university professor?"

"I did—and she said she'll try to get a Robogals chapter started."

Raina slowly shakes her head, wearing a gigantic smile. "How'd you get so brave?"

"Hanging out with my nerd friends." Jamie fist-bumps both girls.

Then she clicks the back arrow and the screen fills with photos from previous summer science camps. "We're gonna have a blast."

EPILOGUE

Soon after grade 5 starts, *Seaker* crosses the border into the U.S. part of Lake Superior. Jamie and her friends check every week or two as the little boat that drew them together keeps journeying farther away, toward the sea.

Jamie is in grade 6 when *Seaker* approaches Niagara Falls. She carefully tracks it, kilometre by kilometre. One evening it's clear the boat will plunge over the edge sometime in the night. Jamie and her friends text back and forth, unable to sleep.

Do you think Seaker made it?

It's been so long now. Seaker must have gone over.

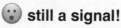 **still a signal!**

The website shows *Seaker* out of danger and entering Lake Ontario. But Jamie doesn't fully believe it until a kayaker comments on the website: "I found your boat washed ashore and returned it to Lake Ontario to continue its travels. Best wishes."

It takes *Seaker* over three years to journey through the Great Lakes. Shortly after leaving Lake Ontario and entering the St. Lawrence River, it stops sending a signal. Jamie and her friends are heartbroken.

Five years after *Seaker*'s launch, when Jamie's finishing grade 9, mail arrives for her. It's postmarked Chéticamp, Nova Scotia. She rips open the envelope and pulls out a photo of a fisherman holding *Seaker*. The boat is faded to pale pink and battered. In shaky printing on the back of the photo are the words, "Congratulations! Your *Seaker* found the Atlantic Ocean."

AUTHOR'S NOTE

I grew up in Nipigon, Ontario, where *Making Seaker* is set. Boats played a memorable role in my childhood, from creating adventures for my toy boats, to independently rowing the narrow red wooden rowboat my Finnish grandfather built, to real motorboat adventures captained by my father. I've loved the *Paddle-to-the-Sea* story since my youth, feeling an affinity to Paddle with his connection to Nipigon and the excitement of discovery in his journey.

Like Jamie, I often puzzled over the endless galaxies of stars, stretching my brain, struggling to make sense of the vastness. When the first moon landing occurred on July 20, 1969, we were on a family vacation, staying at a motel in Gananoque, Ontario. I was ten, going into grade 5 like Jamie. My sister and I were having great fun in the outdoor pool when my mother told us to get out and come watch the moon landing on the black-and-white TV. I've never forgotten that thrilling experience.

I started writing computer code in a high school math class (using keypunch cards!), then studied math at the University of Waterloo, often one of the few female students in my classes. After graduating with a Bachelor of Mathematics with a major in computer science, I worked as a software developer, including several years with MacDonald, Dettwiler and Associates, a Canadian company then involved in developing earth-observation satellite systems.

The classic book *Paddle-to-the-Sea* by Holling Clancy Holling was published eighty years ago, in 1941, and remains in print. I encourage you to check it out! The book inspired Bill Mason to create a short film adaptation of the story called *Paddle to the Sea*, released in 1966, which you can find on the National Film Board of Canada website (https://www.nfb.ca/film/paddle_to_the_sea/).

The book also inspired the creation of Paddle-to-the-Sea Park in Nipigon, officially opened in 2016, that is a collection of interactive play spaces retelling Paddle's story in Ojibwe, French and English.

The park was built with the hard work and support of community volunteers, led by the Nipigon Economic Development Committee.

In *Making Seaker*, while Robogals is a real non-profit organization run by students, the email interaction I wrote and details about setting up a chapter are fictional. Also, I simplified *Seaker*'s tracking equipment and the process of purchasing components; in reality, most items would need to be purchased online. For more information about *Seaker*, tracking equipment and Jamie's real-life science and space inspirations, visit www.seaker.ca.

ACKNOWLEDGEMENTS

My first thank you is to Sumiye Sugawara, librarian at the Nipigon Public Library, for requesting a picture book for a story walk, then offering suggestions for a theme. My deep thanks to Holling Clancy Holling for the beloved *Paddle-to-the-Sea* story that inspired this one.

My original picture book story grew into a chapter book (thanks to a manuscript evaluation by Debbie Rogosin at CANSCAIP's Packaging Your Imagination in 2016), which grew into a short novel (thanks to a manuscript consultation with Harold Underdown), which then expanded until it became the novel in your hands thanks to the insightful and talented editing of Melanie Jeffs at Crwth Press. Each draft of *Making Seaker* improved thanks to the skills and vision of my amazing critiquers: Will

Autio, Stefan Autio, Loraine Kemp, Eileen Holland, Patricia Fraser, Leeann Zouras, Lisa Dunlop, Cris Riedel, Alyson Greene, Michèle Griskey and Mary Ann Thompson. Helpful feedback was generously provided by my beta readers: Marian Petkau, Peyton Dumont-Saunders, Sasha Barber and Shyloh and Piper Wilson.

I'm grateful to each person who answered my research questions and/or reviewed the manuscript or portions to ensure details were correct: Will Autio and Doug Wilson (technical information); Wayne Holland and Sarah and Ryan Traintinger (police details); Jim Failes (science and space information); Jo-Ann Matiachuk and her research group of Asian friends (Chinese-Canadian details); Kellie Wrigley, Principal, George O'Neill Public School (school details); Shy-Anne Bartlett, Interim Indigenous Education System Principal, Superior-Greenstone District School Board (Indigenous content).

My heartfelt thanks to my husband, Will Autio, for his unfailing enthusiasm for my writing and support in my author journey. I'm grateful for the reader-friendly book design and the striking cover that speaks to the STEM aspects of my book, created by Julia Breese; the thorough and thoughtful copy editing by Dawn Loewen and the meticulous proof-reading by Audrey McClellan (our seventh book together!).

ABOUT THE AUTHOR

Karen Autio is the author of numerous books for children, including *Growing up in Wild Horse Canyon* and *Kah-Lan and the Stink-Ink* from Crwth Press. Karen grew up in Nipigon, Ontario, and visits the town almost every year. Today she lives in Kelowna, B.C.

To learn more about Karen and her books, visit www.karenautio.com.